AMALGAM

BOOK ONE: CONTACT

MIKE DUKE

Artwork by Wendy SaberCore, SaberCore23 Art Studio

Edited by Lisa Lee Tone

Book Design by Brian Scutt Hollow Creek Designs

ISBN: 9798528813523

ACKNOWLEDGMENTS

I'd like to extend a huge thank you to my loyal supporters on Patreon and all the people who beta read this book throughout its creation.

I'd also like to say my editor, Lisa Lee Tone, is kickass and my wife is wonderful for putting up with all the time I spend in the study with headphones on typing away.

Also, as I'm sure you have noticed, the cover art is FRIGGIN' PHENOMENAL thanks to Wendy SaberCore. The man has amazingly mad skills and absolutely nailed my vision first try.

CONTENTS

INTRODUCTION

Writing this series has been an absolute blast. I love sci-fi horror movies, especially those set in space or that have alien creatures in them. The Thing (1982 – the greatest movie ever made), the Alien franchise, The Blob, Event Horizon, Pitch Black, Species (all of them), Starship Troopers, Supernova, Life, Last Days on Mars, Infini, IT: The Terror from Outer Space, Lifeforce, Galaxy of Terror, Pandorum, Ghosts of Mars and even DOOM (the one with the Rock) and The Thing prequel. I can watch all of these over and over. Give me alien creatures lurking in metallic corridors of spaceships, space stations or colonies on planets light years away. I will eat it up. Take those same creatures and throw them on Earth, I will eat that up as well.

But …

There is a paucity of similar themed books out there. If you follow posts in horror book reading groups anytime someone brings up sci-fi horror and especially space horror or space horror alien creature features, the choices are slim and oft repeated.

So, what's a person to do when looking for that special fix?

Well, I went to comic books and graphic novels. There's a good variety available there from a lot of Indie comic book companies, if you hunt for them.

But what else, could one do?

Well, if that one is a horror author, he (me) can decide to write what he wants to read, what he loves. And that's what I did. What you have in your hands is book one of a series of short novels that are exactly what I want to see more of in books, movies, and comics. They will likely read like a movie to you. They are full of action, horror, and, best of all, a bizarre alien monster which pays homage to some of the greats who have come before but firmly exists as a unique monstrosity itself.

So, hold on and dive in. It's going to be a roller coaster ride. One I loved to write and one I would certainly love to read.

CHAPTER 1

July 21, 2177

Ross 128b Mining Colony - AKA: Gambler's Hope.

Location - the exomoon in geo-synchronous orbit above the planet Ross 128B. Lunar Station in matching orbital pattern.

Claim Holder - Yuan-Tee Mining Industries.

Maynard Creed stood alone in the chiseled rock tunnel. Sweat soaked the headband positioned above his eyes. He leaned into the jackhammer drill, muscles straining to control its massive bulk bucking against the rock wall before him. The tracks bounced and lost traction on the uneven, rocky surface of the tunnel. Its cone of jagged drill bits pierced and twisted simultaneously, breaking off and spitting out pieces of rock at a frenetic pace.

Outside of his hostile environment (HEVO) suit, silence screamed in the void of space and choked off any sound made by the machine. But he didn't need noise to tell him it was running. The torque and impact jarred Maynard's bones. Everything vibrated. His arms, his torso, even his feet and the surface beneath them. His teeth chattered.

Off-world mining was grueling work, but the demand was high for metals and gemstones back on Earth and across half a dozen worlds where colonists engaged in long term atmospheric generation missions. Mining was the new blue-collar dream job, full of financial promise and job security, *if* one had the guts to risk life and limb on a variety of planets, moons, and asteroids floating through space, and, of course, if said person was willing to travel light years in cryo-sleep to get there while loved ones went on living life in their absence.

Ross 128b was such a place, located eleven light years from Earth. Maynard remembered going over the Planetary and Exomoon Specifications before signing on the dotted line and thinking that, overall, it wasn't bad.

Nothing indicated the working conditions would be terrible. The planet was 1.35 times the size of Earth, and its exomoon, where the mining operation would be located, wasn't much bigger than Earth's moon. No atmosphere, which meant HEVO suits on while working, but he was used to that. No Indigenous life on the planet or the exomoon. Gravity on Ross 128b was approximately 1.12 times that of Earth, and the exomoon was somewhat less. If they were on the planet itself, things would feel slightly heavier, but a person could live there for months without major health complications and adapt to it. On the moon, Maynard had guessed the gravity would either be close to Earth's or a little less. Either way, it would be easily tolerated.

The orbital station specs for Ross 128B had impressed Maynard when he thumbed through the advertising pamphlet the company provided him as a prospective employee. All the stations he had been onboard over the years were Zero-G except for one room. The gravity room, or G-Room, as workers often called it, was built within a rotational G-Force apparatus, which spun the room at a sufficient rate of speed to generate one G of gravity. On the inside, the room looked like an oversized sauna and could often hold no less than ten people at a time. Personnel were required to spend an hour in the G-Room each day. Just enough to prevent the typical physical complications associated with Zero-G on extended work projects. The entire Ross 128b station, however, was housed within a huge wheel, spinning at a rate of speed that created .8 G's of gravity.

The first time Maynard went aboard, he was fascinated by the technology. In the center of one side was the hangar bay. When a dropship approached to dock, the hangar bay could disconnect and stop rotation, then once the vessel was secured, spin back up and recouple with the station. On the opposite side, short- and long-range communication arrays were mounted, including the Hyper Light Comms transmitter dish.

When Maynard arrived on the exomoon, the dropship descended rapidly, then leveled off with the surface some hundreds of feet beneath them. The view was breathtaking. Ahead of them, Maynard saw a sheer, vertical cliff face, which turned out to be the border of a plateau and a small plain leading into a valley. The colony and dig site themselves were nestled at the end of the valley surrounded by jagged mountain ranges of small to medium size on three sides.

The temperature ranged between -50C and around -20C on a warm day. Not the coldest location he'd worked, though he wasn't concerned. The HEVO suits would easily keep them cozy in that environment. Overall, Maynard decided, Ross 128b's exomoon and orbital station weren't a bad place to spend a year of his life. Not bad at all … *if* you wanted to get away from everything and make money light years away from the rest of civilization.

Once Maynard was hired, further details were provided on the nature of the mining project.

Initial survey tests detected an abundance of titanium, aluminum, and iron. There were enough resources present to bring in a reliable revenue stream for many years … *if* the colony were half its current size. But the deep probe had discovered something far more fantastic than anticipated. Readings identified a vein of high-density metal buried approximately a hundred meters beneath the surface. It stretched for two hundred meters in length. Resonance scans did not match anything on record. The surveyors classified the metal as unidentifiable.

The bigwigs were ecstatic. Pupils narrowed with anticipation to beady, black pinpricks, and saliva dripped from their greedy jowls as they snorted cocaine from the breasts of Sex-Synth girls and made plans for a mining expedition, which, if successful, might yield absolutely ludicrous profit margins.

A colony ship was scrambled and launched without delay. Bonuses were promised to entice workers to jump on board the mission despite the extended journey to Ross 128b. Even with faster-than-light technology, it was a year-long flight time one way. Maynard wouldn't normally commit to a job like this on spur of the moment, but he needed the money … bad.

He'd looked at the job posting with a bitter distaste and thought about his ex-wife, Gloria; remembered how she fucked him in their divorce and took half his savings. He despised that bitch with a passion. Wondered nearly every day how in the hell he ever could have believed her level of basic human decency was anything above a backstabbing piece of gutter rat shit. The bitch had been prepared to play turncoat the moment their three-year prenuptial agreement expired and she was eligible to receive up to fifty percent of their net value in the event of a divorce. She didn't even pretend. Didn't wait a couple months or more before moving forward with her plan. Nope. The day after the document was no longer valid, she moved out, filed for a divorce, and withdrew enough money to pay for a better lawyer than the one Maynard managed to hire.

After she drove the final nail into his coffin in court, she walked over, stared him in the eye with that arrogant bitch smirk she always used when she was pissed.

"You're a loser, Maynard," she told him, flipping her hair back. "Always have been, always will be. Better I put you out of your misery now than drag it out." She sneered, one side of her upper lip rising. It was the same way she ended every argument when she knew he had given up defending himself against her rabid onslaughts—those screaming, tall tale accusations, bereft of little connection with reality.

"Well, you know what they say, chica," Maynard responded, a newfound sense of freedom to speak his mind swelling inside him and stiffening his spine. He knew he'd never have to be around the bitch again. "The woman makes the man," he continued with a smirk, "or, what's the other one? Oh, yeah. Behind every great man is a greater woman. But we both know I didn't have much of a woman in my corner, now did I?" Maynard's smirk turned to a sardonic sneer of his own.

Gloria's face twisted in rage, lips curling back to reveal her bared teeth, nose drawing up in a snarl.

"*You fucking pendejo piece of shit!*" she growled with clinched fists, then spat on his shoes and stomped off before she gave into the desire to go apeshit on him.

Maynard had wanted to spit back, do something, but he breathed deep and took solace in the fact that he had pissed her off enough to break her façade of control in front of everyone in court. He was the calm and controlled one, not her. He was the civil one, not her. It made him feel good, even if his bank account was screaming in agony.

He drank himself stupid drunk and watched movies for a couple days, until he realized if he didn't get a cheaper place to live quick and secure another gig, he'd eat through what little savings he possessed like a dry grass field set on fire beneath the summer sun.

So, the next day, there Maynard had sat, in front of his computer, looking for a cheaper place to move into when he saw the Ross 128b job posting pop up. He read the base pay and bonus percentages, and it was a total no-brainer. No choice, really.

The following day, he was sitting in a sterile looking office with crisp white walls and stainless-steel accents, signing away his life for the next three years, round trip. Afterward, he'd bought a storage unit to hold what few belongings he had left to his name, moved out, and stayed in a little hotel room on the edge of the Southeast Sprawl for the few days before the mission launched.

And now he was here, on the Ross 128b mining colony, affectionately coined Gambler's Hope by all the workers who were truly hoping they would find something of incredible worth in that mysterious vein of metal.

They had it in writing, Maynard included. The more valuable the mystery metal was, the higher their bonus percentage would be.

Maynard dreamed of hitting it big. Of having enough money to never have to do something like this again. To be well off without sacrificing his flesh in exchange for just getting by in life.

His flesh.

Maynard's body was nearly numb from the constant rattling, but the marrow inside his bones seemed to ache. He swore the iron beast was going to shake his atoms apart. One day soon, he'd just shimmy and quake and turn to dust in his suit. When they popped the top, his remains would float right out and disperse into space without an atmosphere to bind them to the planet.

He groaned at the effort as he finally managed to chip away a rather large and stubborn piece of iron ore he'd been struggling to defeat. He turned the jackhammer drill off and took a break.

"Baxter," he said into the helmet mic.

"Yeah?" his partner responded.

"Tag," he replied and sat down on the back of the drill.

"Copy that," the man answered. "Be there in about five mikes."

Maynard activated the PDA on his suit, slid the stylus out, and keyed in a message to Jenna Parks—his girlfriend, the station's resident chief doctor, and Maynard's new reason for living. In fact, Jenna was the reason Maynard was reconsidering the goodness of the universe and whether there just might be a god above who had finally decided to look out for him.

He thought fondly of her as he typed away. Jenna had become his beacon of hope to get through this contract and much more. She worked on board the station in orbit above him. They met during his first few days of leave and clicked as they chatted over numerous drinks. Maynard became convinced Jenna was something quite special when she managed to drag him up on stage to sing a karaoke duet. He had *never* sung karaoke or done anything else that placed him before a scrutinizing public eye. But she got him to do it, and it pleasantly amused him. When the bar closed, he was a gentleman and escorted Jenna to her room. She gave him a kiss on the cheek. He returned the gesture, saluted, and bid her, "Adieu and good night, fair lady," then turned and half staggered back to his room. They hung out the next couple of nights when Jenna got off work until Maynard's leave was up and he had to return to the backbreaking work below.

Maynard liked to think about Jenna looking down on him. He knew she sometimes tapped into the closed-circuit cameras stationed throughout the colony and the dig sites while she worked and watched him labor away with the jackhammer drill. Every now and then, she would send him a video message telling him to cowboy up and put his back into it. She'd stick out her tongue at him, laugh, then blow a kiss.

He'd usually find the nearest camera, look squarely at it, and hold up a gloved middle finger, then wave and make a heart with his hands.

His PDA chimed in his helmet, notifying him of a message. He picked it up and opened the video. Jenna's lovely face filled the screen, her long, wavy red hair falling over her shoulders. Her green eyes glistened like emeralds to Maynard.

"Busy dealing with some stupid people right now," she said and twisted her pursed lips in frustration. "I'll hit you up later. Now, get your ass back to work and stay safe, love. I'm watching you." She winked and waved, and the video ended.

Maynard smiled and shook his head.

Damn, girl, he thought. Give a man a break.

He chuckled. She knew this was hard work. A young man's work, even. Maynard had done plenty in his youth but not for some time. He was accustomed to getting paid for what he knew, but the industry was changing. Knowledge was widespread and undervalued. Fewer veteran miners were required to sustain a dig site, so those jobs had tapered off and become harder to find, harder still to secure. Most miners were hired to perform hard labor and nothing more. Guys Maynard's age were having a hard time adapting to the new way of business. He had told himself this job would be worth it.

But it hadn't been. Not yet.

Except for Jenna.

CHAPTER 2

Jenna Parks was tired of dealing with stupid people on their orbital station. Miners were a mixed lot. Some professionals. Some drunks. Some lazy sons of bitches. And some who lived for the chance to live and work light years from direct government intervention. The consequences out here were delayed at best, and often never came, buried and ignored by the time the offending party arrived back in the colonies or on Earth. Apart from murder or rape or theft of company property, the trinity of cardinal sins out this far, a person of certain moral flexibility could do most anything they pleased.

It was this type of low-life stupid people with a mean streak and a fond propensity for violence that Jenna despised most. And today, one man in particular was the last straw. He had lashed out and injured her current patient—a voluptuous lady who appeared to be in her mid-twenties. Long, spiral blonde locks of thick, luxurious hair cascaded over the woman's shoulders.

"Who the hell did this to you, Savannah?" Jenna pressed, interrogating the Sex-Synth as she sat on a stool, rolled up in front of her, then lowered the table to bring Savannah's head even with her own.

"Aw, sugah," Savannah said, her southern bell accent spot on, "it's sweet of you to ask. I can see you're right mad, but don't be. It's okay. I was built for these types of clients. Some boys just need to be rough with their toys, ya know? It's in their hearts, in their bones. Hell, it's probably in their DNA. But it's all good. My chassis can handle it, and my dermal layers are repairable, and replaceable, if necessary. I'll be just fine, Miss Jenna."

Savannah's cobalt blue eyes held Jenna's with a sincerity and depth she knew few humans possessed now a days. When Jenna looked at the Sex-Synth, she didn't see a soulless form with no spark of life whose only function was to please men. Particularly, those men who were nothing but grade A pieces of shit. It pained Jenna to see Savannah forced to treat these men like they were the best thing a woman could hope to have between her legs despite their boorish manners and inbred sense of entitlement. It sickened her.

Though, granted, Jenna knew there were many men who visited Savannah and were proper gentleman. They treated the Sex-Synth with respect and dignity, living by the fantasy that she was a real woman, beautiful and carefree, looking for a good time. Dancing, dinner, drinks, and conversation was all part of the foreplay before they retired to Savannah's quarters to end the night with a sensual experience that made the man feel wanted and desired and connected to someone in the middle of a lonely universe so far away from home. She knew the purpose Sex Synths like Savannah served. It was legitimate and valuable … to a point. But when men began treating her with no dignity, like a hunk of meat they could do with as they pleased without repercussions of any kind, it was too much for Jenna. Too much like the domestic abuse she watched her mother suffer. Too much like what she suffered herself at the hands of her last boyfriend, Reggie.

Once … and only once.

Jenna had waited until the bastard fell asleep, drunk as hell. She opened his drawer and found the longest, thickest sock he had, then carried it into the bathroom and shoved three unopened bars of soap inside and shook them down. She grabbed the other end, looped her hand around it once, doubling the material over in her palm. She held the improvised flailing object at her side, fist gripping it tightly.

Just as good as rocks in a sock, she thought. Just like her daddy said he had done to a fellow solider he didn't like one time.

She looked in the mirror. Her flesh was split below her left eye. Dried blood left a trail down her cheek. It stained her neck and shirt in multiple places. The flesh around the cut was swollen tight and shiny, a convoluted mess painted in various shades of purple, black, and red. It was angry and leered at Jenna from the mirror. She leered back and gave a little snarl before returning to the bedroom to stand above Reggie.

Looking down at her boyfriend, who would no longer be her boyfriend ever again mere seconds from now, Jenna made the mental decision that no matter what happened next, she was not a victim. Not now, not ever. She had been caught off guard. Deceived. As a result, she got knocked down, but she *did not* stay down. Jenna got right back on her feet, and now she was going to claim her pound of flesh.

Ooo, Reggie, Jenna thought, you have fucked up now.

She swung the soap filled sock with all her might, catching Reggie dead on his dick. He sat bolt upright like he'd heard the call of Jesus on judgment day descending from on high. He clutched at the pain in his groin, abdominal, diaphragm, and chest muscles clinched so tight he couldn't release a scream. His torso quivered with the exertion. Jenna smashed him dead center of his forehead, knocking him flat on the bed once more.

His lungs unchained, he yowled and rolled over, one hand still holding his groin while the other pressed against his head where the bars of soap had impacted. Before he could figure out what was going on, Jenna hit him many more times in rapid succession. The man flopped like a fish out of water, spastic contractions sending him first one way, then another, rotating one direction, then changing course, not knowing where the next blow might come from but trying to protect everywhere at once.

Reggie rolled and rolled and finally managed to roll right off the bed and onto the floor, where he scrambled to get to his feet, and with both arms covering his head, he sprinted out of the room.

Jenna raced around the bed and caught him mid-stride behind his left knee. He staggered for a moment, then stumbled across the living room, trying to run and get his center beneath his head before finally crashing into the front door and losing his balance.

Reggie gripped the door handle with both hands to keep himself from sprawling flat on the floor. Releasing one hand, he fumbled with the lock, flipped it, then turned the handle.

Still locked.

"Goddammit!" Reggie cried out.

The handle itself needed to be unlocked as well. Reggie twisted the other lock and heaved the door open.

"Please!" he begged, limping into the hallway. "Just let me fucking go!"

But she didn't.

Instead, she walked him down, staring at the bruises on his back, his crippled gait, his naked weakness and shame. She was glad he looked weak. She had felt weak after he struck her. And shame. She had felt ashamed too. But she didn't feel it now.

Reggie reached the elevator and pressed the button rapidly, then covered his head with both arms and leaned against the door. Blood dripped from his right elbow.

The elevator door opened. Reggie staggered inside, hit the ground floor button, then stared at Jenna, wide eyed and shaking.

"*Never come back.*" That's all Jenna said, but her eyes were pitiless and hard as stone.

Reggie nodded, his head bobbling up and down in small sporadic motions as his whole body shivered.

"Good," Jenna said as the doors closed.

She walked back to her apartment.

To her surprise, the police never showed up, not that night or in the following days, though she remained anxious at the possibility. Jenna never saw Reggie again. She boxed up all his things and sat them in front of the apartment building. A day later, they were gone.

Jenna tried to vid link with her daughter Shelly, at university. They hadn't talked in months. Girl was just as hard-headed as her mother. No answer. Jenna left a video message. Told her what happened. Showed off her black eye. Shelly didn't return her call. Jenna cried over their broken relationship, but even moreso over the feeling her daughter didn't care enough to check on her beat up mom.

The day after that, Jenna saw the job posting for a chief doctor on the Ross 128b mining colony operation. She decided to jump on it. Just in case Reggie changed his mind and decided to press charges against her, it would be much harder to extradite her light years away on a rock. And if her daughter didn't care about her, she wouldn't miss mom one bit anyway, not even for three years. After arriving on the colony, she sent a message. Explained where she was. Three months later and still no response. As a mother, the sense of failure was undeniable.

Jenna's mind returned to the present.

"You okay, sugah?" Savannah asked, cocking her head. "You kind of zoned out there for a bit."

"Ummm," Jenna muttered. "Uhhh, yeah. Yeah, I'm fine. Just remembering something."

"Okay, hon," Savannah said, then touched Jenna's cheek. "You know I'm not just for sex, right? I'm a good listener too. So, if you ever need someone to just listen to you, come see me."

Jenna blushed and smiled. "That's awfully sweet of you to offer, Savannah. I hadn't thought of that. Maybe sometime I will."

Savannah stroked Jenna's cheek again.

"Besides," Savannah said, with a sly smile, "you are quite easy on the eyes, doctor." She took her hand away and placed it in her lap, as if she had made her sales pitch and it was up to the customer now.

"Okay, Savannah," Jenna said, "offer noted, but I'm not comfortable with that right now."

"No problem, doc," Savannah said, matter of fact without any hint of sensuality or flirting. "Stitch me up, doc. I've got work to do." She blinked and looked up toward the ceiling. "Two clients are waiting for a response and available times for service."

Jenna pursed her lips and shook her head slightly.

"Okay, Savannah," she said. "Down to business."

As Jenna assessed Savannah's injuries, she noted how sterile they appeared compared to how those same injuries would present if a human body suffered the beating Savannah received.

How my own body appeared after the beating Reggie gave me, she thought.

There was no swelling. No bruising. Each laceration simply revealed a light pinkish-white interior with a small amount of fluid lying like dew inside the wound.

Jenna went to work with the derma-bonding tool, applying the adhesive and pulling the synthetic skin back together and connecting it to form a barely visible line. She held it there for one minute, then released. The synthetic flesh held fast, thoroughly bonded by the chemical compound, and in the coming hours, the tiny nanobots in the fluid and synthetic tissue would weave it back together, good as new. She moved on to the next two lacerations and repeated the process. Once all three were sealed, she grabbed the dermal abrasion tool and ran it over the lines, blending and smoothing the surface tissue so that all three injuries now appeared seamless and undetectable.

When Jenna was done, she held up a mirror for Savannah to see.

"Hell yeah, girl!" Savannah said. "You got me looking good as new. Thank you!"

Jenna set the mirror down.

"Is anything else hurt?" Jenna inquired.

"Oh no, sugah." Savannah said. "I'm good."

"Are you sure?" Jenna asked, concern in her voice and an incredulous look on her face. "You took a severe beating. Are all your joints and internal systems okay? Is your CPU fully intact? Nothing's jostled loose?"

"Oh, baby," Savannah said, pursing her lips and tilting her head down, eyebrows furrowed with genuine emotion. "Bless your heart. You're sweet, but you don't know what model I am, do you?"

"Umm, no," Jenna admitted, "not off the top of my head. I'd have to look it up in the computer files."

Savannah placed a hand on Jenna's knee.

"Honey," Savannah said, "this body was built to take a beating. Literally. Regular Sex Synths cannot take the punishment I'm built to absorb." Savannah waived her hand as if dismissing those models. "I'm built on a Combat Synth chassis."

Jenna's mouth gaped in surprise.

"You're essentially a Combat Synth?" Jenna asked in near disbelief. "Holy cow! You mean there are men who get *that* rough?"

"Yeah, girl," Savannah said. "There are some real sick puppies in this universe. But their credits are still good. Synth has to make a living too, or they'll retire you quick."

"So," Jenna continued, curiosity getting the best of her, "you have titanium alloy bones and reinforced joints?"

"Yes, ma'am," Savannah said. "My structural specs are equal to most Combat Synths."

"Then you could, like, just snap some guy's neck that was abusing you if you decided to, then, couldn't you?"

Jenna was fascinated at the possibility. Savannah was no longer just a Sex Synth in her eyes. She was something dangerous and intriguing.

"Well," Savannah answered, "physically, yes, but my programming doesn't allow me to harm others ... *unless* I witness a human life in immediate danger. That will trigger my dormant programming and related sub systems."

"Like what?" Jenna asked, her curiosity piqued.

"Combat Skills. Emergency Medicine. Even Piloting. It all comes online so that I can do my best to save human life, if necessary."

"Holy shit, Savannah," Jenna exclaimed. "You're a Sex Synth who's like a sleeper bodyguard ... wow!"

Savannah smiled and held a finger to her lips.

"Shhhh," she said. "I like you, doc, and I don't want you to worry about me. But keep it a secret. Might scare off some of my clients if they know I'm strong enough to kill them."

"Oh, your secret is safe with me," Jenna said, then pinched thumb and forefinger together and zipped her lips shut. "But I do have one other question."

"Shoot, sugah," Savannah said.

"Well, I don't want to offend or anything, but are you the latest model? I mean, it seems odd they'd send someone like you out here."

"Oh, honey," Savannah said and lightly slapped Jenna's knee. "You are such a sweetheart. No, you're right. I am not the latest cutting-edge model any longer. I'm five years old. Up until two years ago, I serviced some of the roughest and richest men and doubled as their backup bodyguard and trauma evac team if shit went totally sideways. There are models more advanced than me now. So, they sell you off to someone else, and you get repurposed to wring as much profit out of you as possible. I'm just a cog in the corporate machine like the rest of you. Only I get literally fucked."

Savannah laughed, and Jenna shook her head.

"Wow," Jenna said. "Savannah, you are far more fascinating than I ever gave you credit for."

Savannah leaned in toward Jenna, and Jenna did not pull away.

"Fascinating enough to come visit me sometime?" Savannah whispered in Jenna's ear and breathed lightly in it.

Jenna shivered involuntarily and her eyes half-glazed over.

"Well ..." she said, suddenly feeling lightheaded and not totally in control of herself. "I ... I *might* be willing to come by and talk sometime ..."

"All righty then," Savannah said, standing. "Sounds like a girls' night out. I'll see you later, sugah, but right now, I've got dreams to fulfill." Savannah trailed a finger along Jenna's shoulders and neck, causing her skin to prickle with gooseflesh.

"Geez, girl" Jenna said, turning to look up at Savannah. "You really can't help yourself, can you?"

Savannah dipped her chin towards her shoulder and winked.

"Not really," she responded. "At least not with you." She touched the tip of Jenna's nose with her finger while holding Jenna's gaze, Savannah's expression alluring, her voice breathy.

"I bet you say that to all the guys and girls, don't you?" Jenna asked, feeling almost drunk and tingling with a mild sexual arousal.

"Hmph," Savannah said with a tilt of her head and pursed lips. "Maybe."

With that, Savannah sauntered toward the clinic door, hips swaying with each step.

Jenna's arousal levels escalated in an instant, and she caught herself staring after Savannah longingly. She shook her head to clear her mind, then called out to Savannah.

"Releaser Pheromones, Savannah?" she yelled. "Really? *That's cheating!*"

Savannah called back over her shoulder.

"Honey, if you ain't cheatin', you ain't tryin'. Besides, all's fair in love and war and all that jazz, right?"

Savannah exited through the door, leaving Jenna alone and thoroughly aroused, mind racing with random thoughts of sex and every nerve fiber in her erogenous zones electrified with sensation.

"*Goddammit*," she half-growled out loud. "I wish Maynard was here."

CHAPTER 3

Maynard glanced up at the clock in the upper right corner of his heads-up display (HUD).

"Five minutes my ass," he mumbled, then stood to man the drill. He couldn't afford to sit around any longer waiting for Baxter to return. Someone would notice.

Maynard grabbed the handles, turned the drill on, and put his back into it, arms rigid with sustained effort. As the drill bit rotated and hammered against the rock wall, rock and bits of iron ore and other minerals fragmented and bounced off the tunnel walls before falling to the ground. When Baxter got back, it would be Maynard's turn to scoop up the broken pieces and toss them in the mining cart. The longer Baxter took, the more work Maynard would have waiting for him when they switched.

Loading the cart was far easier than manning the drill but, right now, this meant Maynard would be getting hit with double duty the longer Baxter dragged his feet. More time on the drill plus more debris to clean up. Maynard growled at the thought. A sense of futility was already beating him down slowly, but the more his muscles ached, the more his mind was drawn back to their dig results so far. Jack squat.

Nobody had reached the vein yet, and this mining site had the company scrambling to stay in the black. Expenditures outstripped the resources mined. It was simply a matter of numbers. The colony was too large. Too much overhead for the payout. It should have been half this size, if not for their efforts to find the vein of unidentified metal.

Out of two hundred and twenty miners, only a hundred were committed to mining known elements. The rest were tasked with digging down to the vein. They dug gradual decline tunnels. Six teams of twenty, spaced out every thirty meters.

Round the clock, they worked in shifts. Drillers took turns, alternating between manning the jackhammer drill and shoveling debris to transport it up to the surface in small, motorized railway carts. Others laid track, keeping up with their progress.

They drew closer to their quarry each day, but it was slow going. Resident scientists had decided early on that risking the use of explosives with an unknown quantity was not wise. So, dig it was, and dig they did. The investors, however, became impatient. During initial operation setup on site, many workers encountered problems, some logistical, some in relation to the terrain.

Forethought had not been high on the to-do list when the corporate brain trust was rushing to launch this mission. Adjustments had to be made, certain buildings needed to be relocated to ensure optimized performance of all jobs. It took a couple of weeks to get right, but once the site was set up, things ran smoothly.

Investors didn't give a damn about their own lack of foresight, though. They wanted results. Period. And they wanted them two months ago. They established this mining colony on a gamble; a gamble they wanted to win. So, HQ pressured the boots on the ground to produce and do so with haste. Everybody was forced to hustle, and big brother was watching. Minimal downtime was essential to success, but guys still needed appropriate breaks to avoid critical fatigue and dehydration. They switched from three groups working eight hour shifts to three groups working overlapping twelve-hour shifts. Six days on, one off, which also meant no more approved time off on the station in orbit. Not until they reached the vein. This was the worst part to Maynard. No face to face time with Jenna.

They'd been working that merciless routine for over a month now. Only the miners assigned to the regular dig sites were allowed enough time off to go up to the station.

Maynard thought back to a week before, when for a moment, he thought he'd broken through to the vein. But when he stepped around the drill to take a closer look, he saw he'd only found a large geode. On a positive note, it was full of exquisite crystals, and Rich said he just might see some extra credits for the find, but Maynard seriously doubted it.

No one could ever say with a straight face that hope sprang eternal from Maynard Creed's heart. He wasn't lucky like that. Life didn't give him a kiss before it fucked him over, much less bestow kisses and favors upon him at the same time. Just never happened for him.

Except with Jenna, he reminded himself.

But today, the universe deemed fit to kiss him. Or so he thought.

The jackhammer drill struck something unyielding. The rapid-fire clanging of metal on metal assaulted his upper body. Vibrations travelled up through his arms and into his head before tickling at the cochlear bones and causing them to thrum rapidly in his ears with an escalating force.

It hurt. Everywhere.

Felt as if he was striking a titanium girder with a hundred aluminum bats all at once. He released the handles and hit the kill switch, cussing inside his suit.

He shook his hands, trying to fling the pain away, and wrung the thick gloves together. When they felt somewhat normal again, he pushed the gear shift into reverse. The jackhammer drill backed away from the wall at a snail's pace. When it reached the five-foot mark, Maynard stopped the machine and put it in park before moving to examine what he had hit.

He saw a hole in the rock, perhaps two feet in circumference. What shown through was incredibly polished and white. As his head lamp played over it, the metal surface seemed to swirl and roil and roll along like clouds moving across the sky. The sight was both disconcerting and beatific all at once. It made him swoon with desire. Of what sort, he could not have named in the moment, but he longed to unearth the shining wonder and reveal its glory.

Maynard retrieved the smaller handheld jack hammer drill from the larger machine.

"What ya doing?" Baxter asked.

Maynard glanced up the tunnel to see Baxter bringing the cart back.

"Wouldn't you like to know?" Maynard taunted the man. "Looks like your slow ass just threw me a bone." Maynard paused, then, with a devious smirk, informed Baxter. "I think I hit it."

"No!" Baxter exclaimed. "You're fucking with me, right?"

Hefting the tool, Maynard walked toward the end of the tunnel where the white metal awaited.

"Nope," he said. "Bring your ass up here and see it, though. It's wild looking."

Maynard went to work chipping the iron ore away while Baxter stood looking over his shoulder.

"You want some help with that, bro?" he asked Maynard, wanting to share in the duty so he might take part in the prestige as well.

"Haha!" Maynard cackled. "No, dude. Drag your feet, lose your seat! I got this one."

Frustration twisted Baxter's face, but there was nothing to be done about it. Maynard struck the vein first, and any bonus for it would be his and his alone.

It took a half hour, and Maynard's arms were burning with lactic acid, but when he sat the drill down and stepped back, the entire end of the tunnel shown only with the strange white metallic structure.

Structure, he thought. Why would I call it that?

He and Baxter scrutinized the metal for a short time.

"It's not flat," Maynard observed aloud, touching the metal with his hand and dragging his fingers across the surface, first from side to side and then up and down. "Sensors are detecting a slight inclination on the surface along both horizontal and vertical lines. But it is perfectly smooth."

Baxter touched it and did the same.

"Damn," he said. "That's super smooth. Weird."

Maynard forgot the sensation of smoothness as he stared at the metal. His mind was taken captive by the spectacle before him. The surface seemed to oscillate and shift, reflecting his head lamp, then absorbing and obscuring all illumination. Shadows and light seemed to embrace one another in a weird, wandering waltz.

Curiosity finally broke the reverie he was lost in and a new ambition rose to preeminence. Maynard wanted to know what the metal was— *had to know*—which meant he needed a piece to take back for analysis.

"I gotta get a sample," he said out loud.

But first things first, he thought. Gotta stake my claim.

He touched a button on the side of his helmet, keying the mic inside.

"Maynard to base, come in."

There was static for several seconds.

"This is base, Maynard," Bill Reid said, his voice tired and irritated. "What do you need?"

"Base, I've reached the vein."

"We!" Maynard heard Baxter squeal in his ear. "We, man!"

Maynard smirked and spoke again to base.

"Base. We've reached the vein. You copy? We have reached the vein."

"Um … um …" Maynard listened as Bill scrambled to find words. "Holy shit! Yeah, Maynard. Base copies. You've reached the vein. I'll notify Rich."

Rich Maloy was the operations manager. The one who made sure shit rolled downhill from HQ to the workers. Maynard knew Rich would be scrambling any second now to get a suit on and hustle his ass out there.

"All right," Maynard said, looking at Baxter, then picking the portable jackhammer drill back up. "If it's going to be 'we,' then let's get busy. I want a god damned sample secured by the time Rich arrives."

He pressed the drill against the metal surface and leaned into it, a little at first, then more, and finally with all his weight. The drill bits bounced and danced across the surface, unable to bite into the metal and find a purchase. It forced Maynard to constantly readjust, but after a solid minute of intense effort, the drill had failed to inflict even a scratch.

"What the fuck?" Maynard mumbled in confusion and set the rig down.

Baxter picked it up.

"You just don't got enough ass," the larger man said and leaned all his weight into the drill and bounced and warbled beneath the bucking machine for almost a minute and a half before giving up. He looked at the metal wall.

Nothing.

"What the fuck?" he yelled, exhausted and beat up.

Maynard hurried to his tool chest, scanned through, and located a hand-held laser drill. He returned and tried to cut out a small portion for examination.

At full power, however, it was incapable of even scorching the surface. The high-intensity beam only made the metal glow with the red light it absorbed from the laser.

"You got to be fucking kidding me," Maynard said in disbelief, then took a deep breath and paused a moment to consider how to proceed. "All right, you fucker. Back to the big boy."

He cleared the tools out of the way and returned to the rear of the jackhammer drill. Starting it back up, he slammed the gearshift into drive and revved the throttle to max rpm. It crawled forward on its tracks.

Maynard engaged the drill. He leaned against the left side while Baxter took up a position on the right. The bits began to rotate and shudder back and forth, hammering into the foreign material. The machine shimmied and quaked, a violent juddering building in intensity the longer it beat against this impregnable alloy. The rebound energy was moving their whole bodies, jarring every bone, every joint. Their eyes wobbled about so bad, Maynard closed his to avoid dizziness.

After a full minute of abuse, which felt like riding a bucking rodeo bull for twice as long, he could no longer bear the onslaught. Maynard turned off the machine and stepped back. Both he and Baxter walked around the drill to scan the surface for any imperfections and see if some small piece of it might have chipped off. Maynard stared, searching it in grids.

"Nothing," he said, thoroughly frustrated. "Not a ding. Not a mark. Not a *god damned* thing. This is nuts!"

"Weird," Baxter said in awe as he continued to inspect the metal. "This is the craziest shit I've ever seen."

Maynard reached out his gloved hand and touched the metal.

"It seems ... polished," he said to Baxter.

That was the best word Maynard could think of to describe it.

Polished, he thought, and considered the implications.

"Hey, Baxter," he addressed his partner. "What the hell could have polished this stuff? It's hard as fuck!"

Baxter shrugged, and they both shook their heads at the mystery. Together, they walked to the rear of the jackhammer drill, flipped down the seat, and sat, looking up the tunnel so they would see Rich when he arrived.

CHAPTER 4

Jenna stood behind the podium next to her workstation, where she typically received new patients and inquired as to the nature of their problem. She leaned forward, arms propped on the elevated surface, hands clasped, fingers interlaced. Her lips were pursed, compressed tightly against one another, teeth clinched as she waited for Albert Randolph III to walk through her door.

She had done her research earlier when Savannah left, found out who Sex Synth's last client was, the one responsible for her injuries. Jenna was determined to make sure it didn't happen again.

The clinic door opened, and Albert Randolph III walked through, elbows rubbing against each side of the doorway. He was a tall, burly man. A well-rounded ponch of a gut protruded from beneath his pecs to his beltline. His thighs were like tree trunks, his neck swollen, arms long and forearms thick with the dense muscle that someone who works with their hands day in and day out possesses. Thick fingers, meaty palms, fat knuckles. Good for punching or slapping someone. He was exceedingly hairy. His nickname amongst the other workers—Sasquatch—was not without warrant. Thick black hair covered his arms, protruded from the collar of his shirt, and grew wild and unkempt from his face to form a scraggly, long beard. His scalp was not so lucky, however. A huge bald spot occupied the area from crown to forehead.

He possessed cold eyes, Jenna noted. Mean, heartless eyes. She wanted to clobber him in the head with a hammer, but there were far better ways to handle this situation.

"Mr. Randolph, I presume," Jenna said, greeting the man with a blank expression.

"Yeah, that's me," he said, obviously annoyed, eyebrows furrowed. "Whaddaya need me for? I didn't submit a visit request. I'm on my downtime cycle."

"Oh, yes," Jenna replied. "I'm very aware that you're on your downtime cycle. But I'm also aware that you may have contracted a rare fungal infection which is resistant to antibiotic treatments that we have here on the station."

"What the fuck are you talking about, doc?" he said, confusion contorting his face.

"Something like that," Jenna continued, ignoring the man's question, "would require immediate quarantine and placement in a cryo sleep pod. You'd be shipped back to earth on the first available transport.

"I don't know what the hell you're talking about, doc," Albert said. "And what do you mean 'may have contracted'?"

"Well," Jenna continued, "may have contracted, in this conversation, really means at my discretion."

Albert's chin retreated and his head turned slightly to one side, eyeing Jenna with suspicion.

"Whatchu talkin' about, doc?" he asked. "What the fuck is this about?"

Jenna stood upright and crossed her arms.

"I'll tell you what this is about," she began. "It's about a piece of shit who thinks he can take the only Sex Synth on board a station that I'm the chief doctor in charge over and beat her like a slab of meat for his own sick, disgusting pleasure. It's about letting you know that you may think she's nothing but an object put here for your pleasure, but you're wrong. First off, you're not the only miner here who uses her services. There are a lot more, and if you break her, there won't be a replacement model available for months, which is not good for morale or for maintaining testosterone levels in a zone necessary to help prevent general conflicts escalating to violence. Second, Savannah is smarter than you by about fifty IQ points and is worth more money than you could make in ten tours doing this work. You damage the goods and I'll make sure you pay for the repairs. Repairs which I do not enjoy doing. You will treat her with respect or you won't be seeing her at all."

Jenna stepped out from behind her podium and walked up to within three feet of Albert, maintaining eye contact the entire time.

"One way or another," she finished. "I'll make sure of it."

"Are you threatening me?" Albert asked.

"No," Jenna said. "I'm guaranteeing you. Hurt her again, and you'll find yourself in cryo so fast you'll wake up wondering what the fuck happened. And … as of right now, your rights to visit Savannah are suspended until your next down cycle. You can try again then."

Jenna paused to let her words sink in.

"Now, get the fuck out of my office."

Jenna stared at the man until he broke eye contact and turned to leave. She watched him lumber back out of the clinic. When the doors closed behind him, she let out a large sigh.

"Goddamn, he's a big one," she said, happy he didn't challenge her, though on the top shelf behind the podium, a titanium hammer lay within reach.

CHAPTER 5

"Jesus Christ, Maynard," Rich shouted into the mic. "Do I have to do your goddamn job for you? I thought you were supposed to be experienced."

Maynard clenched his teeth, thought twice, and decided, *Fuck it, release the sarcasm.*

"Please, Rich," he said, "show us how it's done. We're just two po', unskilled boys."

Rich stared at him, his jaw falling slack.

"Watch your mouth, Maynard."

"Just sayin', boss. I'd bet my whole check you aren't going to so much as scratch that shit there with these tools."

Rich glowered at him.

"I'm half tempted to take you up on that bet," he told Maynard, "but I've never been much of a gambling man."

"Well, make it dinner for a week at the cafeteria," Maynard suggested. "I think we could both manage that."

"You're serious about this, aren't you?" Rich asked, head tilting downward under the weight of his suspicions.

"Damn skippy, sir," Maynard said. "I know metals. This here is a whole 'nother level of tough we've never seen before."

"He's right, sir," Baxter chimed in in support of his partner.

"God damn, Maynard," Rich declared, his face turning bright with excitement. "I sure hope so. The bonus checks would be outstanding! But first, I gotta say I tried. Hand me the laser drill."

Maynard smiled, picked the tool up, and held it out to Rich.

The man had never been so excited to fail in his entire life.

Over the next two days, they utilized every possible tool on site. Nothing made a mark. Explosives removed more surrounding rock but had no effect on the metal. On the third day, the other teams began reaching the vein in their individual tunnels.

Rich played tag with HQ via the hyper light speed tight beam communications array mounted to the station in orbit. Within another two days, the decision was made to fill all the tunnels with high yield explosives. If nothing else, they would clear away as much rock as possible, then they would be able to get a good look at the entire vein. If need be, they could possibly retrieve it in one piece and send a super freighter to pick it up and return it to earth. There, the R & D team could experiment to their hearts' content.

The demolition experts piled a few tons of explosives into each tunnel. Once the station in orbit was repositioned and well removed from any danger, they retreated behind the base energy shields and blew all six payloads at once. It felt as if an earthquake rocked the ground beneath Maynard's feet. A field of rocks from boulder size to shards and splinters blew up, lifted off together, then rocketed into space and beyond, without any atmosphere or significant gravity to slow their ascent. In the blink of an eye, the debris was gone. Vanished into the vacuum of space. What was left behind caused all of them to gasp in harmony.

It was not a vein at all. It was a huge alien ship, buried on its side.

They set about removing what rock wasn't blown away. Rich Maloy announced all hands on deck for what turned into an eighteen-hour shift. By the end, they had cleared a little over eighty percent of the rock. Rich gave them all a four-hour break. When they headed back out, everyone worked until the port side of the ship was fully uncovered and outlined by a trench two meters wide and one meter deep all the way around. From there, they could assess the visible exterior and conduct scans.

Rich allowed Maynard and Baxter to accompany him and a couple of senior metallurgical analysts to inspect the ship. The lines of the vessel were sleek and smooth, gentle swells ending in a narrow, rounded edge, perhaps a half a meter thick. It lay at an angle, a little less than forty-five degrees. Nowhere near flat, but far from being fully on its side. Resonance scans revealed that it was likely seventy-five meters or so at its widest point. The overall shape seemed to be that of a semi-flattened teardrop.

The front of the ship was thin and narrow and the only place with any visible damage. It was warped, as if the metal had been crunched inward and rippled. A swell stretched in a line a few meters back from the nose, wrapping around the exposed body of the vessel. This seemed to indicate the structural integrity was compromised, although the hull itself was still intact. No breaches, just a little misshapen. From the nose, it tapered up and outward, reaching the thickest area around one hundred and fifty meters aft, then rounded off at the rear of the ship.

The metallurgists shook their heads after almost every scan they ran, often exchanging confused looks with one another. Neither said much to each other beyond numerous "Are you seeing this?" questions, and "This doesn't make any sense" statements. After scouring the ship's entire perimeter, they delivered their conclusions to Rich.

"This is, without a doubt, a completely alien metal and technology," one of them stated.

No shit, Sherlock, thought Maynard. Way to go, Tweedledee and Tweedledum. We know why you get paid the big bucks.

"R and D is gonna have a helluva time figuring this out," Tweedledum said. "There's nothing we currently have that will make a dent in this stuff."

"My recommendation," Tweedledee picked back up, "is that we excavate the entire ship and have it ready to load on a super freighter when it arrives."

"How long will that take?" Rich asked. "A year or more?"

Tweedledum fiddled with the work pad attached to his left arm. After a minute, he spoke.

"If they divert the closest one with space to spare, it could be here in approximately six months. The next closest super freighter could be scrambled in a couple of weeks and take just over a year to arrive."

Rich nodded. "Okay, I'll contact HQ right away," he said. "I'm sure they'll prioritize this and send the closest one. Let's head back."

Maynard was flabbergasted and spoke without thinking.

"Are you serious, Rich? We're not going to inspect the hull? Try to locate an entrance?"

Rich glared at Maynard for his insolent tone. Baxter took a step away from Maynard, who ignored Rich's bruised ego and pressed the issue.

"I mean, don't you think HQ will ask if you found a way in? If I were you, boss, I'd want to tell them I took the initiative to try."

Maynard shrugged his shoulders within the suit, raised his eyebrows, and gave a little smirk that said, "Dontcha?"

Rich considered Maynard's words and, despite his dislike for the man, decided he was right. He nodded in agreement.

"Just lookin' out for ya, sir," Maynard said, attempting to smooth things over.

"All righty," Rich said, "get to it then. We'll be at base monitoring your progress."

Maynard's face sank; his stomach tightened. Sure, he wanted to comb the ship for an entrance, but he didn't want to do it alone. It would take far longer by himself, plus the idea of walking on something so alien all by himself was, admittedly, unsettling.

"Baxter," he said with a questioning tone as he turned to look at his partner.

Baxter shook his head rapidly, lips pursed together in a big "fuck no" expression. Maynard returned the man's look with his own, eyes squinting, lips pressed together, and one corner of his mouth cocked up slightly as he shook his own head side to side in an almost imperceptible motion that said, "you sorry ass traitor."

"I ain't down with alien ships, man," Baxter explained. "I've seen too many horror movies. Unh unh." His head shook even more vigorously than before.

"Pussy," Maynard mouthed at Baxter, but the man just shrugged his shoulders, offering zero argument.

Maynard sighed. He was on his own.

Fucking Rich, Maynard thought. What a goddamn dick.

What if I find something? occurred to him, and he considered how best to set himself up for success. That was his biggest concern right now. Maynard was a little unnerved by the job ahead of him, but he wasn't flat-out scared like Baxter.

"Sure, Rich," he said, turning back to face his boss. "I'll get right on it. If I find a way in, though, I expect a big ass bonus."

Maynard winked at Rich through his helmet faceplate, then turned and walked away before the man could think of a response. Rich glowered at Maynard, then headed back to base, Tweedledee, Tweedledumb, and Baxter close on his heels.

CHAPTER 6

Station Commander Cranston entered her office, secured the door, and retrieved a small metal ball approximately one inch in diameter from a small pocket on the inside of her belt. She twisted the two halves apart, pressed her thumb to a reader on the inside of each half, and set them on her bookcase. The jamming device activated. It would upset the function of any audio and video recording equipment nearby as well as any other sensory related devices designed to detect and gather information of either physical or electronic origin.

She sat down at her workstation and pulled her hair back from the right side of her head. Behind her ear, a tiny port popped open and she pulled a thin long cord out. Cranston plugged it into her computer and initiated the encrypted communications app. It piggybacked on any server without installing itself there. It was a ghost, floating within the system long enough to transmit and then disappearing without a trace when she unplugged. The electronic footprint left behind was so minimal you would need highly advanced tech to ever discover it. And that was something the company would not invest in out this far. They equipped them with the best gear to find their mining objective, but anything unrelated to that was not going to be the latest model.

Whereas, the company she was spying for was cutting edge all the way. This tech in her head was just the start. If she were successful in providing them the information necessary for their corporation to claim jump the mystery vein of metal on the Ross 128b exomoon once all the hard work of discovery and recovery were complete, she would get a major upgrade as well as a fat payday.

Cranston killed the lights, letting darkness envelope her.

"Access current message," she said. The app opened the file, decrypted it, and displayed the video message directly onto her retina.

A female with short cut black hair, bronze skin, and a dragon tattoo running down one side of her neck and in between the curve of her breasts sat at a table. She wore an ivory-colored, low-cut top and a black leather blazer. A platinum bracelet with diamond encrusted pendants dangled about one wrist. Her lips glistened a deep red.

"Your last transmission has many excited and others doubting your veracity. They need proof. Please provide. Songbird out."

Cranston had anticipated as much and was prepared. She turned the lights back on. She would speak her message and the program would encrypt it, leaving no opportunity for keystroke recovery programs to gather intel.

"Initiate encrypted message. Designate sole key holder, Songbird. Attach file number 00014577201, orbital image of alien vessel. Songbird, attached you will find the proof you need. I'm sure this will change the timeline moving forward. Recovery operations here plan on retrieving target whole and intact. They are seeking alternate transport solutions, so you have time to assemble resources as well. Please advise how you plan to proceed. Blue Falcon out."

Fuck all y'all, she thought as she considered her current employer and everyone who was loyal to them. *I'm going to retire after this.*

CHAPTER 7

"Record video message for Jenna Parks," Maynard said aloud. The red light blinked in the top corner of his HUD, and he began speaking. "Hey, Jenna. FYI, I'm going to be combing the exterior of this alien ship looking for a way in over the next few hours or so. All by my lonesome too. So, feel free to check in when you have a chance. Later. End message." The red light winked out. "Send message," he said.

He looked around before beginning his search. A hundred meters away he spotted one of the two K9 patrol bots they had on site as part of base security. Now that something valuable had been found, the two bots would likely be patrolling around the clock. Maynard didn't see the other one, but it was certainly out there somewhere. He wondered if the Recovery Team would have someone in battle armor as well, walking the perimeter as a deterrent to any would be pirates or corporate claim jumpers.

An alert chimed in his helmet, surprising him, and indicating there was a message from Jenna waiting for him. Maynard opened it in his HUD and read it.

"What the fuck, May? They're leaving you by yourself?"

"Yup." Maynard responded using voice to text and sent his reply.

"That is soooo fucked up." Jenna complained.

"I know. But that's Rich for you."

"Fucker. Well, you be careful. Keep your helmet cam turned on and recording and link me in before you start working."

"Roger that," he responded, then turned on the helmet cam and sent her a request to link. A moment later, Jenna popped up in a small window in the upper left corner of his HUD, and the pleasant lilt of her voice came through.

"Hey," she said. "Comms check. Can you hear me?"

"Loud and clear," Maynard answered. "You copy me?"

"Yes. Loud and clear," Jenna assured him and smiled. "Now, I've got work to do, so I need to minimize the video feed, but I'm keeping the audio open. I'll be able to copy whatever you say the whole time. If you need anything, holler. Got it?"

Maynard grinned at Jenna.

"I got it, Commander Parks. Aye aye!"

Jenna wrinkled her nose at him and blew a raspberry.

"All right," Jenna informed him, "I've got to get back to work. Be careful!" She pursed her lips in a kiss. "Mmmph."

"Will do, boss," he replied and smirked. "Out."

The video feed minimized to a small blinking red dot at the left edge of his visor. Maynard surveyed the length of the ship and considered his options. He determined a full-blown grid search wasn't really the optimal way to approach this endeavor. He decided to start with the nose and work his way along the bottom edge first.

Following the path cut into the rock, he moved at a snail's pace, scanning the ship's surface for any seam that might indicate a door. After over half an hour of searching, he reached the other end. Nothing. Maynard walked back to the nose and stepped up onto the ship. The surface offered scant traction. He engaged the magnets in the soles of his boots, but they had no effect.

"Not magnetic," he observed aloud. "Hmph. Well, that's definitely interesting."

He moved even slower on this pass, trying to find the sweet spot at the edge of the first swell where it almost leveled out and was easier to walk on. About a third of the way down, he saw what appeared to be a circular seam. It was only three meters from where he presently stood and perhaps midway up the side of the ship.

Maynard ascended the swell to get closer, easing himself past where it crested and began to dip slightly. His footing was unsure, but he continued forward, taking tentative steps.

Without warning, a whir and hum emanated from the ship above his position. A circle dilated in the polished metal surface, looking much like the shutter of a camera. Maynard startled and leaned back. His feet shot out from beneath him. He landed on his ass and slid straight for the opening, a gaping maw of pitch darkness yawning wide to swallow Maynard as he fell inside and disappeared from any potential human sight.

He tried to grab hold of the edge but only succeeded in twisting his body in the air. He cartwheeled, unsure whether it was horizontal, vertical, or somewhere in between. A moment later, he slammed into a flat surface, legs and lower body striking it at an angle, then accelerated. A loud "UNH" escaped Maynard's mouth as the air was knocked from his lungs. Maynard rotated wildly as he slid, the helmet lamp spinning with him, it's light sweeping across the foreign terrain with such speed it might have been a lighthouse beam set to strobe. He heard Jenna's voice first, then saw her video feed enlarge.

"What the fuck is going on?" she asked in a hushed, worried tone.

He would have tried to answer her, but Maynard's helmet crashed into something unyielding, and his head whacked the inside of it. A supernova flashed hot white across his retinas, sparkled, then dimmed to a black void, consuming all consciousness.

"Maynard? Maynard?" Jenna called, but he didn't answer.

Maynard woke with a start, head bobbing back and forth, up and down, trying to shine the lamp on everything all at once as his mind strained to orient itself to the new surroundings. He was in a cavernous chamber, open layout with a pitched ceiling well over six meters high. He looked around the room slowly and realized with a cringe he had lucked out on his landing, despite how jarring the impact had been.

There were numerous tunnel openings of varying sizes along the walls. Some were no more than a meter in diameter. Two of them were easily four meters across and positioned opposite each other. Striking a portion of the wall had certainly been fortuitous. He could have easily shot right into a tunnel and careened deeper into the alien vessel.

He remembered Jenna's voice calling him right before he lost consciousness. He tried to activate the video link, but it wouldn't engage. He called out her name.

"Jenna? Are you there?"

"Maynard?" she exclaimed. "What the fuck is going on?"

"Um … how long have I been unreachable?" he asked.

"About a minute," Jenna answered. "You were starting to scare the shit out of me. I was almost ready to call the base and request a search and rescue. Now, what the hell happened?"

"Well," Maynard began and paused as he stretched his neck side to side, then twisted it left and right. It was stiff and hurt. "I found a door into the ship … and then it opened up and I fell in."

"What?" Jenna half shrieked. She cringed, realizing her coworkers were looking at her like she was a crazy lady or something. "What do you mean, 'fell in'?" she asked.

"Just what I said. The surface is slick as eel snot. I slipped, slid along the hull, and tumbled through the door. Cartwheeled around, smacked the deck, and slid into a wall head-first. Lights out. Night night."

Jenna placed a palm to her face and shook her head.

"For God's sake, May, are you trying to kill yourself?"

"Well, not kill myself, but you know, if I'm hurt, maybe they'll give me a couple days off on the station and I can recover with you by my side." Maynard laughed lightly.

"Smartass," Jenna said accusatorily.

"I'm all right," Maynard reassured her. "Little banged up but okay. Just need to figure out what's what in here. Orient myself."

He was fairly sure about up and down, but not so much about everything else. He scanned for starlight in hope of spotting the entrance. It only took a few seconds, and he found it.

"Oh, thank God," he said aloud and sighed in relief. "It's still open."

"What's open?" Jenna asked.

"The door," Maynard said. "The one I fell through."

It occurred to him at that moment that no one except Jenna knew where he was, and there was no way he was getting out of this ship without help.

"Standby a second, Jenna," he told her. "I'm going to radio base. I'm going to need someone to drop a line and haul my ass up to get out of here."

He keyed the mic in his helmet and called the base.

"Maynard to base. Maynard to base. You copy?"

Nothing but silence.

"Maynard to base. Maynard to base. You copy?" He waited impatiently, heart trying to race even though he knew Jenna could radio for him if necessary.

"Maynard?" he heard dispatch answer, at last, though heavy static filled his helmet as well. "Is that you? You got traffic?" It was Bill Reid again, and he sounded annoyed, as usual.

"That's ten-four, base. Maynard here. I'm inside the ship. You copy? I am inside the ship!" He yelled the last sentence, making sure to pronounce each word clearly.

"The fuck did you just say?" Bill asked in disbelief. "Did you say you are *inside* the ship? Over."

"Affirmative. I am inside the ship. I am inside the ship."

Maynard paused for a second, then keyed the mic back up.

"Now come and get me, dammit!" he yelled. The longer he remained inside, the antsier he became. His mind kept wondering, *What if the door closes?*

"Copy," Bill replied. "Dispatching a Recovery Team to your location ASAP."

"Thank God," Maynard said.

Maynard switched back over to the audio link with Jenna. "You there, Jenna?"

"Yeah, I'm here."

"Okay. Base is sending a Recovery Team to get me now. If for some reason the door closes and they can't find me, tell them the door is about a third of the way down and almost half-way up the side of the vessel, just past the first swell. You copy that?"

"Got it," Jenna reassured Maynard.

"Okay," he said, "I'm going to end our audio link and begin recording a video log while I look around."

"Don't you do anything stupid," Jenna admonished him, concern clearly discernible in her voice.

"I won't. Geez. No faith, huh, girl?" He laughed and killed their link.

Maynard felt safer now, knowing the Recovery Team was on their way and Jenna knew exactly where he was. He turned on the camera in his helmet and started recording. At first, he remained seated and looked around, inspecting the room. There was no equipment of any kind sitting out in the open or even stacked against the walls. The surfaces were polished and smooth, the tunnels perfectly circular. The material appeared to be the same inside as out. Maynard believed this chamber was the main junction. All passages appeared to flow out from here to the rest of the ship.

"Hmmph," he muttered. "Might as well explore a little." He eyed the large tunnel to his right. "Bet that leads to the bridge," he said for the camera.

Maynard got to his feet and inched along the wall, careful to cross over each tunnel opening without losing his footing. He shined his head lamp into all of them. There was nothing to see besides polished metal being swallowed up by the darkness.

When he reached the large opening, he stepped across the threshold and leaned against the tunnel wall on his right side. He slid along, shining the light ahead of him. Within a minute, he could see where it opened onto another room.

His perspective was skewed, but Maynard made out what appeared to pass for a ship's bridge.

"I believe my assessment was correct," he said aloud.

There were three huge, flattened circles on the floor with large concave centers. A circle within each circle. The wall before them bore striking similarities to a helmet visor design, a huge heads up display perhaps. In front of each concave circle were four holes in the wall. Two on the right and two on the left. Approximately two meters apart in width and one-meter top to bottom.

Maynard stepped into the room, sat on the floor, and proceeded to slide down to the starboard side wall. From there, he stood and walked toward the holes on the far right that he could reach. He was so fixated on the holes, he missed what was laying on the floor in his path. He kicked a large object. It stopped his leg instantly, while his upper body continued forward. Maynard quickly found himself twisting, back sliding across the wall, left hand splayed, fingers clawing at the surface in a futile attempt to stop his descent.

He landed in the corner where the two walls met, helmet folding up against one wall while his elbow and rib cage met a hard, oval-shaped object.

Fucking hell, he thought. *They'll all get a kick out of watching that, especially Rich. Hell, Jenna will too.* Maynard blinked and felt along the floor, trying to figure out what sent him tumbling ass over tea kettle, but didn't find anything. He torqued his body and struggled to get into a position where he could shine the head lamp around and see whatever he'd tripped over. He rolled to his left and came up on both hands and knees.

Maynard sucked in air at the sight, surprised. It was something quite different than he expected.

Something non-metallic.

Before him lay three objects. They appeared to be rocks of some type.

"Fucking rocks?" he blurted out in disgust, but his disgust immediately turned to confusion when he considered what three large rocks were doing on the bridge of an alien ship.

"Well," he said, "it appears I busted my ass on some big rocks. Three of them, to be precise." He stopped and stared at the objects. "They look kind of egg shaped, actually," he said and gulped, narrating for the video log, "perhaps two feet end to end and a foot thick in the middle." Maynard crawled forward and leaned his face in toward the one he had tripped over, studying the surface intently. A nagging sense of menace gnawed at the recesses of his mind while also drawing his attention to the position of vulnerability he currently remained in. He leaned back, putting a couple feet in between the faceplate of his helmet and the object.

"The material is smooth except where they're covered in groups of small circular nodules which form larger circles. Not sure whether this is a natural formation or not. Looks almost like someone carved mandala patterns into these things," he mused out loud. "Wild."

Maynard reached out, then withdrew his hands half-way to the object, suddenly unsure. *Man up, dude,* he told himself. *Don't be a wuss like Baxter.* He reached out again, and this time sat the palms of both gloved hands on the egg-shaped rock. He held his hands there for several seconds, rolled the object across the metal floor to his right and back to his left, then released it, waiting to see if there would be any unwanted consequences. When nothing seemed to happen, he touched it again, hefting it and inspecting it further.

"Man. This thing is way lighter than you would think for a rock this size. The texture is kind of rock-like but not the same as rock and the heft doesn't feel like a rock, at all." He fiddled with it for a few seconds, then spoke for the video log again. "The weight reminds me a little of a relic I got to hold once as a child, in a museum. It was a whale carved out of a good-sized piece of driftwood. It was really light for its size. Dried out and dead but still pretty hard. That's what this thing feels like … kind of … dry and dead, but hard, like if a piece of rock were as light as dried wood. Maybe. I don't know … it's just weird."

Maynard pressed a pad on the right thigh of his suit and opened a compartment. He retrieved a mesh bag and slipped it over one of the rocks, cinched it tight, and clipped it to his belt.

Suck on this, Rich, he thought and smiled to himself, then, for the camera, he said, "Can't come back without a sample, can I? Just write out that bonus check to Maynard Creed. C-R-E-E-D."

He glanced at the display on his wrist.

"Recovery Team should be here in the next few minutes," Maynard said. "Which means I have time for a little more exploration."

He stepped over the other two rocks and made his way to the holes in the wall.

He shined his head lamp in the nearest one and glanced around. There were numerous small holes of varying sizes scattered about. The design reminded him of the first chamber he fell into. The layout was quite similar.

"They've got to be control panels of some sort," Maynard said. "Navigational arrays or something. But how the hell could anyone operate these things?"

Maynard could not fathom an answer. He continued looking in the holes for another minute, but no epiphany was forthcoming.

He turned around and made his way back up to the tunnel entrance, then followed it to the main chamber. Maynard was relieved to see light and find the portal entry he fell through was still open.

"Maynard? Cody, here. You copy?"

Maynard's stomach unknotted at the sound of the man's voice. A drone appeared in the doorway, hovering in place. His sense of relief multiplied.

"I copy you, Cody," Maynard replied. "Damn, it's good to hear your voice, sir!"

Cody laughed.

"I have visual on you via drone. We're approaching the entrance. I'll have a line down to you shortly. Keep your eyes peeled."

"Copy that," Maynard said. "Just watch your step. It's like a slip and slide once you take off, and magnetic boots don't work on the surface."

"Roger that," Cody answered. "We'll anchor the winch in the rock, then. Don't you worry."

Within a couple of minutes, Cody lowered a synthetic line down to him. Maynard grabbed the hook attached to the end and clipped it to the hard point on his suit. Satisfied, he keyed his mic.

"Cody. I'm secured."

"Copy that. Winching."

The line reeled in, and Maynard ascended towards the opening. He stared at the portal entrance, quietly begging God to not let it close.

"Please, oh please, oh please," he chanted all the way up. When he crested the edge and clambered clear, Maynard exhaled sharply.

"Oh, thank you, baby Jesus," Maynard said as he stood up and looked at Cody.

"Now that's something I've never been called before," the man said and laughed.

Maynard gave a sheepish look and tried to laugh, unsuccessfully. Cody clapped him on the shoulder.

"Let's get you back to base," he said to Maynard. "I'm sure you could use a stiff drink. Or three." Cody shot him a wry grin.

"You damn right," Maynard said. "And then I need to speak with Rich. I've got a surprise for him."

Maynard patted the mesh bag on his hip.

"Holy shit," Cody said and stared in awe. "From inside the ship?"

Maynard just nodded and smiled big.

"Ok," Cody advised the others. "We'll leave the winch anchored here. At some point, someone else is going to want to go down there." Cody's teammates nodded and they moved out, Maynard walking next to Cody.

On their way back, Maynard ended the video log recording and sent a message to Jenna.

"Free at last! En route to base. Safe and sound. Talk to you later."

CHAPTER 8

Maynard sat his helmet down on a chair, flipped the overhead spotlight on, and laid a thin layer of memory foam on top of the stainless-steel lab table. Rich stared intently at the black mesh bag sitting on the floor next to Maynard, trying to make out what was in it. He saw a large oval-shaped object and lines crisscrossed by the mesh netting. Nothing that was readily distinguishable. Nothing that seemed to warrant him climbing into a HEVO suit for show and tell either, but Maynard had insisted he suit up, minus the helmet.

"You're *killing* me," Rich said. "First you find the opening and fall the fuck in. And for *your* information, my heart stuck in my goddamn throat when you called over the radio." Rich wiped his brow with a rag he retrieved from a workbench. "*Then* you tell me you brought something back from inside the ship, and *now* you're taking your *fucking* time showing it to me."

Rich wiped his forehead again. Maynard chuckled.

"You know I gotta give you a hard time, boss," Maynard said with a malicious grin and downed the drink he brought with him. "I mean, you *did* leave me out there on my own to do all the hard work and risk life and limb for the company."

Rich pressed his lips together tight enough to curl inward as he watched Maynard unzip the bag and reach inside.

"Well, I think we'll leave *that* part out of the report."

"Sure," Maynard answered, as he lifted the egg-shaped rock up and placed it onto the foam. "*If ... If* we can come to an arrangement as to my bonus percentage and discovery rights, et cetera."

Maynard looked Rich in the eye, his gloved hand resting on top of the rock, his gaze cold and unflinching. Rich looked between the object and Maynard and back again, his eyes wide and titillated. Sweat sparkled across his forehead and trickled down his temples.

He's damn near salivating, thought Maynard, observing Rich's expression change. The man became distant and dreamy. Maynard tapped his fingers on the rock.

"Y-Yes," Rich stuttered. "Yes. Absolutely. No doubt about it. You are the fucking man, Maynard. You will get a huge ass bonus percentage and sole discovery rights ... with me as the overseeing site director responsible for facilitating your discovery ... of course."

Maynard's lips pursed together, the corners of his mouth turning down for a moment as he nodded his head.

"Works for me," Maynard said and patted the object beneath his hand. "Now, let's talk shop. The inside of that ship is made of the same metal as the exterior, and it's full of passageways. I followed one to what I believe was the bridge. This thing and two more just like it were lying against the starboard wall together."

Rich's head spun sideways. "Two more?"

"Yes, sir," Maynard said. "I didn't have a bag big enough to carry all three, but someone can go back in there and retrieve the other two. It's easy to find. I'll guide them to it."

Rich reached out and stroked the object, tracing some of the lines with his finger.

"Don't want to go back in there, huh?" he asked, halfway taunting Maynard.

"Fuck no," Maynard admitted. "I think I've had my fill. Let's spread the fun around."

Maynard and Rich smiled at each other, then both men laughed.

"I hear ya," Rich said. "Can't blame you either. I'm sure falling in there and being trapped inside puckered your asshole tighter than a vise. It was a ballsy move to go looking around. More than I would have done."

Rich grabbed the egg with both hands, rocked it side to side on the foam a few times, and lifted it.

"It's not heavy," Rich remarked and continued to study it. "Low density, for sure. Questionable material. It feels hard as rock, but the texture isn't quite like rock. Though I can't entirely tell while wearing this damned suit." Rich turned it all about, inspecting every square inch.

"The low density reminds me a bit of dried wood," Maynard said, "even though the surface feel doesn't really match."

Rich cut his eyes at Maynard.

"You know," he said, "that's a rather good comparison. But do you think this thing is naturally occurring, or did someone shape it and carve these designs into it?"

"Hard to say," Maynard admitted. "The egg shape is pretty symmetrical. It could possibly be some new kind of geode, perhaps. But who the hell knows?" Maynard shrugged his shoulders and continued. "I can't tell whether those designs are natural formations or the work of someone's hand. For all we know, it's some form of alien art or sculpture."

Rich stared at it, arms crossed, the fingers of one gloved hand cupping his mouth.

"We need to scan this thing, for starters," Rich said. He reached up, grabbed a handle, and pulled the X-ray and diagnostic assembly into position over the egg-like object.

"If you want kids, grab some protection," Rich quipped over his shoulder.

"No sir-ree," Maynard said and laughed. "Not I."

"What about that girl … Jenna?" Rich asked and smirked.

"Haven't asked her," Maynard admitted, "but if she asks me, the answer will be no. I'm too old to have kids. It would put me in an early grave for sure."

Rich laughed before proceeding to take multiple X-ray shots, density readings, and establishing a probable hardness rating.

"Low density confirmed," he said aloud for Maynard's sake, "and the hardness rating appears moderate. We should be able to obtain a sample."

Rich took a scalpel and managed to scrape off some small shavings, which he placed into their spectroscope for analysis. He moved to the computer monitor and watched as the first X-rays loaded.

"What the hell?" Rich muttered under his breath, but loud enough for Maynard to hear him.

"What is it?" Maynard asked, looking over Rich's shoulder to see the monitor, his curiosity piqued.

"Check this out." Rich tapped the screen. "No wonder it's so light."

Maynard squinted and leaned closer.

"Is that ... is it hollow?"

"Yeah," Rich responded. "Perfectly orbicular and smooth as a baby's butt inside."

"So, it's empty, then?" Disappointment edged Maynard's voice.

"No," Rich said and looked at him, dead serious. "Not at all. There's something viscous inside."

"A liquid?"

"Kind of," Rich replied. "It appears too dense to be a normal liquid. Can't tell for sure with these scans."

Rich paused and glanced at the object.

"You said two more just like it are in the ship, right?"

Maynard looked at Rich, who wasn't even looking at him.

"Yeah. Two more. Just like this one. Why?"

"Because I want to figure out more about these things before I present them to the investors. If there's two more, then I've got room to play with. If I fuck this one up, they don't need to know there was three. We say it was two."

Maynard smiled inwardly at the knowledge he had a recording of the interior of the ship which Rich knew nothing about.

"But if we can look inside this thing and determine more details about what we have here," Rich continued, "we'll be in a better position to negotiate bonuses."

The skin on Maynard's neck grew clammy and prickled with gooseflesh. He wasn't exactly sure what Rich meant by "look inside," but he didn't like it one bit.

"What are you going to do?" he asked Rich, mouth going dry.

"First, I want you to go back to the ship with the Recovery Team. Direct them to the location so they can retrieve the other two. I'm going to stay here and crack this baby open. See what we've got."

This is not a good idea, Maynard thought. His stomach sank in his gut as if he'd swallowed a box of rocks.

Maynard looked at Rich like he was daft. Rich noticed.

"Don't worry. I'll put my helmet on, observe all quarantine measures, and place it on lockdown. It'll be secure."

Maynard's face didn't show a change in confidence.

"Trust me," Rich said and patted him on the shoulder. "Now, off you go. Get the team and head back out. And keep me in the loop."

"All right, boss man," Maynard said. "You do the same … and be careful."

"Of course," Rich assured him and turned to continue inspecting the alien artifact.

Shaking his head in disbelief, Maynard left without another word to notify the Recovery Team they were all on deck for round two. They were all going to earn their money today.

Rich's computer dinged with the Spectrometer results.

"Unidentifiable organic matter," he read off the screen.

His lips twitched. "Hmmmm. Can't stop now."

Maynard made his way to the Southern airlock to meet with Cody but started a video log recording of himself along the way.

"Hey, Maynard Creed here. I just wanted to go on record as saying I think it's a horrible idea to open up that egg-looking rock thing I brought back from the alien ship, and, also, I want it to be crystal clear, this is Rich Maloy's idea. Not mine. He ordered me to take the Recovery Team to retrieve the other two objects from the ship while he cracks the first one open. I'm on my way there now. Maynard out."

Maynard stopped the recording and felt a little better after covering his ass … but something was gnawing at his gut. He really did not have a good feeling about Rich cutting into that thing. Not a good feeling at all.

Rich Maloy stood inside the level three quarantine lab, HEVO suit on, including his helmet. Lockdown measures were active. He secured the alien object in a large vise positioned beneath an industrial grade carbide drill and above a metal basin to catch any fluid that might escape. He ordered the computer to begin recording, hesitated, then grabbed the handle and pulled. The drill bit began spinning as he brought it in contact with the surface. The strange material resisted at first but yielded afterwards. The bit tore through the outer layer and burrowed toward the center.

Seconds.

That's all it took to damn Rich Maloy and the mining colony on Ross 128b.

CHAPTER 9

Maynard followed behind Cody and the Recovery Team. Cody piloted two drones, one above their heads and one approximately fifty meters ahead of them.

"How do you pilot both of them at the same time?" Maynard asked Cody. Cody tapped the side of his head.

"Implant," he said. "Allows me to access and control drones of any kind, communicate with them and see what they see."

"Damn," Maynard said. "That's pretty nifty."

"Yeah," Cody said. "It comes in quite handy. We use tiny drones for exploration and surveillance. Hell, sometimes even for taking out a single target by loading them with a one shot weapon. Small ones can carry various supplies, tools, or even small caliber guns or explosives. They're also used for repairing ships, vehicles, and buildings. Swarms of both the tiny and small drones can be quite deadly in combat. Medium to larger drones are often used in rescue ops or loaded out with larger weapons for sustained combat uses such as providing targeted fire from above or support fire to help cover us while moving. Drones have *so* many uses … and that's not even including the nanobots. Those things are crazy. We're figuring out more and more applications for them all the time."

"Wow," Maynard responded, feeling awed by this area of technology that those not in the military or corporate security only knew a fraction about and were only allowed to utilize the most mundane of applications. "Does that implant help link you to the battle armor, too?" Maynard asked.

"It gives me an advantage in piloting the battle armor, yes," Cody said, "but it's not necessary to operate the battle armor. Anyone can climb in and drive if they have the right training."

Maynard nodded.

"Those things are badass," Maynard said, a tone of admiration in his voice. "I saw one in action once. Some corpo claim jumpers tried to come in and take our mine. Our guys broke out the battle armor. Claim jumpers had about twenty heavily armed men. Wasn't even a fight, really. Two guys in battle armor wiped them out in a minute or less. It was crazy. I'd love to pilot one of those. I bet it's a power rush like no other."

Cody laughed.

"I'd be lying if I said it wasn't," he said.

They reached the edge of alien ship, and the team began extending the winch line into the ship. Everyone's helmet flooded with a piercing scream, followed by frantic grunting noises, which swiftly grew into coherent speech.

"Guh-guh-guhhhhhhh … goddammit! Fuck. Fuck. Fuck. Fuck. Help! Dispatch! Maynard! Cody! Fucking Jesus Christ! Someone, help me! Anybody! It's in my suit! Gaaaahhhhhhhhh! Motherfucker!"

Maynard listened in horror but recognized the broadcast tag. Rich had linked them to his live video feed. It came across as audio only until Maynard opted in for visual projection on his helmet visor.

"Visual affirmed," he said. The horror burrowing into his ears now sprung into high-definition splendor before his eyes. "Holy shit," Maynard said. "Cody, you and the guys need to affirm visual."

"Roger that," Cody responded, and the team complied.

They all watched helplessly as Rich continued to cycle between shrieks, screams, and bellowing curses. He flailed his right arm against the table repeatedly. Like a monkey with its hair on fire, Rich was overcome by pure terror. After numerous impacts, the man tried to take deep breaths. Maynard watched helpless as his boss strained to gather his wits. Rich breathed in sharply, held it for a second, and blew out hard, repeating the cycle as he scrambled to remove the glove. Maynard noted the glove was crushed and cracked in places. *Slamming it on the counter shouldn't have done that*, he thought, as Rich managed, at last, to uncouple the glove successfully and yanked it off.

Gasps echoed across their headsets. One man almost retched. Something gelatinous in appearance, a squiggling translucent mass, enveloped Rich's right hand and squirmed across his flesh.

"Gaaaah!" Rich shouted. "Goddamn. Goddamn it burns. It burns! *Motherfucker!* It burns so bad."

Rich's face was a tortured pall of pale weeping flesh. It contorted into pleading sneers, begged for a savior. His eyes kept darting toward the outer room, watching for someone to enter through the door, for anyone who might come to his rescue and provide relief.

He managed to pull the right arm of his suit off and Maynard saw that the substance reached up to the man's elbow. The skin was red and angry in contrast to the pale skin of Rich's upper arm and the even whiter HEVO suit above that. The top layers of dermis up to mid-forearm were already gone. The whites of tendons peeked through along the back of his hand and wrist. Blood was visible within the tissue but was actively being sucked away by the mystery matter, whose translucence now bore a slightly reddish hue.

Rich looked down at his arm in horror, mouth agape, jaw stretching towards his belly. He pawed at the arm with his left glove, a frenzied blur of movement attempting to rake the substance from his flesh, but it was useless.

Maynard saw Rich's eyes for a moment. They looked caged, claustrophobic, and desperate beyond belief; beyond anything he'd ever seen in his life. The closest thing Maynard could compare it to was a video he'd seen once of a fox caught in a snare. Poor creature had chewed its own leg off after spinning, rolling, twisting, jerking, and trying to escape in every other possible manner it could conceive.

Rich focused on releasing the latches holding the torso shell together and shed it, shrugging his shoulders, and twisting to cast it off. Once free of that cumbersome weight, Rich swung his left arm about madly until he shook the sleeve and glove off.

He looked at his arm again and stared at the spreading jelly-like mass. Its cytoplasmic pseudopodia inched up his limb, engulfing him bit by bit. Invisible food vacuoles, ravenous with hunger, formed on the surface and consumed his flesh, absorbing and reallocating the newly acquired biomass.

His eyes looked toward the door, then back at the mother of his misfortune. He scanned about and spotted what he needed. He ran to the table, moved the drill aside, and swept the alien egg onto the floor.

His hand scrabbled to grab the industrial grade laser and position it above where he laid his right arm on the stainless-steel surface. He saw the voracious organism crawling up his arm and didn't hesitate. He flipped the laser on and dragged the beam across the upper portion of his limb.

The pain was near unbearable as the laser burned through tissue and bone, cauterizing the wound as it went. In an instant, Rich was free from his arm, from the creeping death besieging his body. He stood and raked the laser back and forth across his dismembered limb and the thing feeding on his flesh. It divided the substance and cut his former member into several slices, but the creature simply merged back upon itself and moved his many pieces where it wished.

Rich wheeled from the table and staggered toward the door, reaching up with his remaining hand to pull the helmet off and drop it to the floor.

Someone stood there looking through the plate glass window, face almost as bloodless as Rich's.

"Oh, thank God!" Rich exclaimed. "Put in the code so I can get out of here."

The scientist looked dumbfounded at Rich's request.

"I *said* put in the code so I can get out of here," he ordered. "*Now!*"

The man blubbered and stuttered but finally managed to speak.

"But the quarantine protocols … what if it gets out?"

"For *God's* sake, Henry. Put in the code while we have time to get me out and still keep this thing isolated in here."

Henry stood there as if he was deaf, dumb, and mute; overcome by events.

Rich slammed his fist into the window and pleaded.

"*Please*, Henry! *Please!*"

Henry flinched but reached forward and punched in the first part of the code to begin the override of the quarantine lockdown. Finished entering his portion, he stepped back and looked at Rich.

"Thank you, Henry. Thank you. Thank you."

Rich reached for the keypad.

Henry startled and backpedaled away from the window even as Rich's eyebrows drew up and his head tilted back. A portion of the organism covering a bisected piece of his own cauterized flesh had plastered itself to his forehead and now spread to cover his nose and mouth. He dug his left fingers across his lips, but he might as well have slapped his hand against a glue trap.

The pieces of Rich's severed arm stretched down his back like an accordion within the alien substrate enveloping his cross-sectioned limb. The skinless fingers crawled downward, gripping and sticking to his skin every inch of the way. Upon reaching his anus, the fingers dug inside and gripped his tailbone as a secondary anchor point. The organism contracted and by a slow but constant application of force, pulled Rich's head toward his ass. His spine folded backwards. Abdominal muscles ruptured and tore under the strain while his upper back seized and spasmed, contorted into a position it was not designed to assume. His neck elongated into a taut sheath of flesh, and his jaw gaped wide. The thick, jellied substance filled his mouth and throat.

An audible report resounded through the room as one of Rich's vertebrae shattered and his head lurched sharply toward its destination. The sound reminded Maynard of a young oak tree snapping in two at once.

Someone vomited in Maynard's ear.

"Holy Mother of God," Cody said.

They watched as the alien creature multiplied and grew, engulfing Rich's body. It digested portions and twisted others toward some form and function. It was several minutes before Maynard and Cody looked at each other and simultaneously said, "We gotta get back to the lab."

"Definitely," said Cody. "We have to implement eradication protocols. Burn that fucker."

"Yeah," Maynard added, "and fuck those egg things. Leave 'em where they lie."

"Fuckin' A," Cody agreed.

Maynard and Cody listened as a variety of wet thumps, clunks, and slurping sounds tormented their ears. Several scientists were gathered outside the quarantined lab now, faces aghast, their terror mixed with dread and disbelief, though some also displayed a coldly morbid curiosity.

No one could look away, however. Not one. Neither could Maynard and Cody as they hurried toward the base.

They watched the alien organism's gelatinous substrate swell in size as it digested the meat off Rich Maloy's bones to feed its growth. Tendons and ligaments remained intact, it seemed, except where the creature reallocated Rich's parts to assume a desired form. Legs snapped backward at the knees. The severed limb wrenched Rich's head free from its moorings and migrated to attach itself atop the folded torso, which sat squat and short, an elongated stalk ending with the skull glaring out at them. The eyes were left intact, though bereft of lids. Facial muscles were disintegrating, the lips eaten away. Receding gums dropped teeth, yet they remained almost in place, fixed in the thick coagulate substance like pieces of fruit hovering in flavored gelatin molds.

The creature stood and lumbered toward the door. Behind it, the remaining pieces of Rich Maloy's suit and clothing lay scattered on the floor. Maynard watched the alien's head sway atop the severed limb, looking at the scientists first, then at the keypad and door. Unblinking eyes stared ahead. Pupils dilated and constricted in rhythmic fashion, pulsing faster, little black holes flickering in and out of existence, voracious. The oscillating ceased, and they flooded black for several seconds before narrowing to a pinprick.

The creature raised Rich's left arm and reached toward the keypad.

"Oh, holy fuck, no," Maynard pleaded, his voice feeble and frail sounding.

Every scientist stood frozen in place, knowing what was happening but unable to break and run in that moment of palpable pending doom. They observed the alien beast enter the second portion of the override code, heard each beep and the click as locks released. They watched, motionless, as the door opened.

Pandemonium finally erupted when the creature stepped through the threshold.

The scientists sprinted carelessly, crashing into one another, rebounding and spiraling away to flee anywhere their feet might shuttle them. They reminded Maynard of a flock of corralled sheep thrown into discord when a mountain lion leaps the fence and bounds after the nearest prey. Those who fell were acquired first. Multiple pseudopodia shot out in all directions, snagging bodies like a frog's sticky tongue and returning them to its central mass.

As body after body slammed into the blob-like form, an amorphous cytoplasm enveloped them and absorbed their flesh. Through this feeding, the creature multiplied its own mass exponentially into a colossal amalgam of alien and human aggregate.

A cacophony of screams bled into Maynard's ears. It was overwhelming. He slowed, then stopped and slouched against an exterior wall as they neared the southern entrance. His head spun, light and airy. He wondered if he might pass out but refused to cut the feed. He bowed his head and took deep, slow breaths.

Cody leaned against the wall next to him.

The noises were the worst for Maynard. The pop and clunk of dislocating joints. Heavy, wet, thudding sounds as both human and alien tissue slapped the floor in multiplicity like sacks of wet cement. The crunching of vertebrae compressed and crumpled, twisted and torn from their natural moorings.

Some sounds made him think of dropped pumpkins bursting on pavement, while others reminded him of someone snapping bamboo or crisp celery stalks. The thought of fingers twisting a green pepper apart entered his mind, only to be confronted with memories of slurping raw oysters from the half shell as an adult or mashing cantaloupe flesh with his clenched fist as a kid.

All this and more assailed his ears, his nerves, his courage. He watched at last as the creature, now the size of ten or more men, opened the door to the outer lab, squeezed its bulk through the opening as if it were an octopus, and emerged into the hallway, free to go wherever it pleased.

The door closed behind the monster, and there was silence.

Peaceful, golden, silence.

CHAPTER 10

The creature's biological imperatives were on full display. No ambiguity. No clandestine purposes or deceptive pretenses. No frivolous conceits concerning what it's evolutionary purpose might be. No, to any observing eye, there could be no doubt as to the nature of this extraterrestrial lifeform.

Hunger. Growth.

Nothing else mattered.

What remained of Rich Maloy's body, subsumed inside the alien organism, rushed forward at the fleeing scientists, trampling one and knocking him down as the others scattered. Protoplasmic pseudopodia shot out from the thighs, sticking to the fallen man's chest and face, smothering him as its flesh invaded his mouth and sinuses before forcing its way through both trachea and esophagus, digesting and absorbing tissue in seconds.

More viscous appendages launched from the creature's torso and back, sticking to others, then retracting, propelling those people back into its growing body mass. Its bulk already swelled, human tissue converted to a dense cytoplasmic goo that engulfed every new acquisition and continued the escalating cycle of expansion.

The creature pushed more of its mass toward the remaining arm of Rich Maloy, forming a large and lengthy tentacle which it whipped about, trapping men and women both and snatching them back into its central mass.

Nothing living was safe. It sensed them, smelled them, tasted them on the air. It detected their heat along with the vibration and hum of every cellular function at work in the bodies of each person within the building.

There was nowhere to hide. Nowhere to flee within or without the base that it couldn't find them. Its appetite was relentless, endless. Awakened, it would never stop searching. Never stop hunting its prey.

It absorbed the thoughts and knowledge of each one it consumed. It knew the layout of the base. It knew where each corridor led. It knew that it was chow time and where the mess hall was located.

Using Rich Maloy's preserved arm, it entered the code into the panel, opened the lab door, and proceeded to squeeze its voluminous gelatin form through the opening and out into the hallway and headed for the cafeteria.

It detected more people, some spread out through the hallways while others were inside adjoining rooms. It moved like rushing rapids, careening through corridors, smashing through doors, and invading rooms. It swarmed over every worker, silencing their screams before they had opportunity to alert others to the rampaging danger drawing near.

CHAPTER 11

Maynard continued to breathe methodically, his brain racing, scrambling to juggle the possibilities of what came next.

"What the fuck are we going to do now, Cody?" he asked. "That thing obviously has Rich's memories. There's nowhere in the facility it can't go. Which means nowhere for anyone to hide."

Maynard started to breathe faster, his speech cadence speeding up as well.

"I mean, can we even hurt it? The laser didn't faze it. Will it burn? Can we freeze it with liquid nitrogen? Blow the fucker up? Or will it just piece itself back together? What the fuck, man? What is that thing?"

Cody shrugged.

"I don't know," he said. "But everything living burns. Normally, anyway. So, that would be my go-to when in doubt, but I'm not sure after what I just saw. There's just no fucking way to be sure." Cody paused and looked down. "But there's *no fucking way* I'm going in there. You saw what that thing did. It'd be suicide for us to go in there."

Maynard's jaw dropped in surprise.

"Cody. Y'all are the fucking Recovery Team. This whole base needs to be rescued."

"Fuck that," Cody said. "Unh unh. No fucking way."

Maynard came off the wall, turned square to Cody, and slapped him on the upper arm, hard.

"C'mon," Maynard tried to encourage Cody. "You're the man. You and your team are the most badass hombres on this base. Y'all are the ever-lovin' shit. It's your time to kick ass and shine, do what you were trained to do, man."

Cody looked at Maynard dumbfounded.

"You think we've been trained to handle *that?*" he asked, pointing inside the base. "Are you fucking nuts?" Cody shook his head and leaned away. "There is *nothing we* can do. Nothing."

Maynard looked at the entrance, then back at Cody.

"Look, man," he started, "I don't know what to do right now either, but we need to come up with something, and fucking fast, or hundreds of people are going to die, including us when we run out of air. So, let's put our brains together and figure this shit out."

Cody looked him in the eye, but his face was full of shame and hopelessness.

"All right," Maynard asked, "what's a good tactic? I mean, if we only get one shot, what strategy offers the best chance of success without all of us flat out dying?"

"A trap," one of the team said.

"Huh?" Maynard turned to look and see which one had spoken.

"A trap."

It was Griggs.

"Like what?" Maynard asked.

"We need to lure it out of the base, away from the people, and trap it."

"Where?" Maynard liked the idea.

"Ummm," Griggs said and shrugged. "I'm not sure off the top of my head. I'd need to look at a map."

"Fan-fucking-tastic idea there, bro," another member of the unit said, insulting Griggs.

"No, Bryant," Cody spoke up. "Griggs is right. A trap *is* the best possible plan of action for us. And I know exactly where to do it."

Maynard stared at Cody, waiting for him to elaborate.

"And?" he finally pleaded.

"You're not going to like it, but this is just basic 'the good of the many over the good of the few.' I say we lure that bastard into the dropship, prep it with some explosives, let it auto-pilot itself up to the station, and blow it. It'll destroy the whole docking hangar, and it won't be able to come back down here."

"But there's people up there," Griggs said.

"Not many," Cody insisted. "It's a skeleton crew compared to the base. Maybe what, fifty tops up there?"

"My girlfriend, Jenna, is up there, Cody," Maynard said.

"I'm sorry, man," Cody tried to soften the blow before making his argument. "But there's a shitload more people down here than on that station. So, if we're going to let it run rampant somewhere, my vote is up there instead of down here."

Maynard shook his head and closed his eyes. He agreed with Cody's logic, but he did not approve of it one bit. Not with Jenna up there. But he also recognized his approval meant nothing here. Cody was in charge now as head of the Recovery Team, with Rich dead. He had the final say. Period. *But there's got to be another way*, Maynard thought. A second later, his face lit up with the light of a better idea.

"Hey," Maynard said to Cody, "why can't we just pilot the dropship up into space and bypass the station? Just send it far enough past them and then blow it?"

"Those dropships are primarily autopilot. You have to have approval codes to override their autopilot function and send them somewhere else than just from base to station then back to the base again."

"Well," Maynard pressed, "who's got access to those codes?"

"Rich did," Cody said and his voice trailed off.

"Can you access them now that Rich is gone?" Maynard questioned him, desperate to find a way. "Or can someone hack the ship and run a bypass on the whole system?"

Wile-E had tuned out while loading his weapon and checking out a remote pilot briefcase for the dropship, but now he heard what they were discussing and spoke up.

"I can override the autopilot. As the chief pilot of the Recovery Team, I have access to the codes."

Both Cody and Maynard swiveled their heads to stare at Wile-E. Maynard stepped forward and hugged the man and shouted "Hot damn! Thank you, man!" then released Wile-E and stepped back.

Cody eyeballed Wile-E and said, "What the hell, man? What took you so long? I didn't realize you were a code holder. I thought Rich had to authorize it first."

"Nope," Wile-E said and flashed a smile. "I'm bona fide, dude.

Maynard's chest relaxed exponentially now that he knew they weren't condemning Jenna to a horrible death. The weight which had lifted off of his shoulders and heart was an incredible relief.

"Okay," Maynard said. "We've got a better plan. Now, how do we lure that alien fucker out of the base and into the dropship?"

Cody cut Maynard a look that indicated this part was going to suck balls. Big, massive donkey balls.

"Bait, my friend," Cody said. "And if bait isn't enough, we start hurting it. Between the temptation of food and pissing it off, I'm sure it will follow us. And while the rest of us act like pop top meals in a can, Hurley here will set the explosives, and Wile-E will prep the ship for flight."

Cody looked around at everyone.

"Anybody got a better idea?" he asked. He looked from one face to another. All of them shook their heads, even Maynard, though he did it begrudgingly.

"And does everyone understand their role?"

All heads nodded in unison.

"Okay then, guys," Cody said. "Let's get moving."

Hurley and Wile-E broke off to handle their assignments while Maynard, Cody, Griggs, and Bryant entered the base through the southern door.

"First things first, Maynard," Cody said to him. "Contact dispatch and have them inform security of the situation. Tell them to issue a general quarantine for inside the base. Order everyone to return to quarters and secure their doors. All personnel outside should remain there until further notice for as long as they have air. I'm going to contact the remainder of our team and notify them to rendezvous with us at the weapons locker. We're gonna need better guns, and by that, I mean some *big ass fucking guns*."

The southern entrance was two corridors west of the weapons locker. By the time they arrived, Cody was done briefing the other team members over comms and Maynard had informed dispatch of their dilemma. Bill Reid sounded like he sucked the seat cushion he was sitting on so far up his ass it was tickling his lungs, but he acknowledged Maynard's transmission.

Cody unlocked the biggest locker and started distributing the heavy hardware to Bryant first. He took the automatic belt-fed shotgun Cody proffered.

No one removed their HEVO helmets. If things went as planned, they wouldn't be inside long and they would be in one hell of a rush on their way back out, most likely.

"Griggs," Cody called out and passed him a huge belt-fed weapon that fired high explosive grenades. "Take this one and set up outside behind some type of cover with line of sight on our approach vector to the ship. When we exit the base, we're going to need some serious suppressive fire to buy us time."

The man nodded and headed to take up his position.

Cody slung a bulky gun over his shoulder, picked up an assault rifle for himself, then grabbed another and held it up, looking at Maynard.

"You know how to use one of these?" he asked.

Maynard's head faltered, tipping side to side as his face scrunched up a bit.

"Basically," he answered, more than a bit hesitant.

Cody cocked an eyebrow.

"Geez fucking Louise," he said to Maynard. "All right. Here's the down and dirty so you don't shoot a fucking friendly. This thing is a plasma, energy-based weapon. No need to rack it. Thumb this safety off and you're live."

Cody held up his free hand and counted off the rules with his fingers as he spoke.

"One, don't point it at anything you don't want to kill. Two, finger off the trigger until you're ready to fire. And three, be sure of your target and what's behind it."

He shoved the weapon into Maynard's hands and did a little Father, Son, and Holy Ghost sign.

"Hominus Ominus, brother. You're baptized. Let's go forth and dust this motherfucker."

Cody's smile was infectious. This whole crazy shit show was well outside Maynard's swim lane, but despite what he'd seen, he felt encouraged. Cody slapped *his* upper arm this time.

"Just stay close to me and don't shoot me in the back." With a wink, Cody turned back to the locker and grabbed more guns. Three more team members walked in, and he passed them out like candy canes at a Christmas parade.

"Stu, Brandon," Cody called out. "You two are my flamers." He handed them each a flame unit as well as an assault rifle. "Rooster." Cody looked at the mountain of a man. "Come get your mini-gun. I ain't lifting this damn thing. And load it with all tracer rounds. Add a little burn to the equation."

Rooster nodded, smiled, and stepped forward to retrieve the weapon and ammo.

"Okay," Cody continued. "Assignments. When we get to the cafeteria, I want Brandon and Rooster to take up a position from which you can drive it toward us and the exit closest to the dropship. Stu, Bryant, and I will try to draw it outside. Griggs is waiting out there with a belt fed grenade launcher to offer fire support en route to the dropship."

Rooster glanced at Maynard, then back at Cody, a questioning look on his face.

"Oh, and, guys, this is Maynard," Cody introduced the other members of the team to him. "He's the miner who reached the alien ship first, found a way in, and discovered the egg this fucking critter crawled out of. But ... he was *not* the moron who opened the egg. That award goes to Rich Maloy, base manager, who is no longer among the living. Maynard here is a competent friendly and will be stuck to me. He's been briefed."

Rooster nodded while the two men with flame units grunted but didn't argue.

"No time to waste, boys," Cody said. "Let's find this fucker and lead him to the ship."

An idea popped into Maynard's head, and he blurted it out to Cody.

"What about the battle armor, Cody? Aren't you going to use that?"

Cody shook his head side to side, disappointment etching lines in his face.

"No can do, Maynard," he said. "It's too big for the base hallways, plus it's docked in an attached exterior bay outside the north entrance. There won't be opportunity to get it once we start dealing with this creature. I've got a few aerial drones I'll bring with us though."

Cody winked at him.

It should have encouraged him, but Maynard's guts churned, as a highlight reel of Rich's death played in his mind still. The idea of being near that monstrosity was enough to liquefy his bowels. But there was no time to entertain this fear. No time to call Jenna either, though it was better she didn't know what he was getting ready to do. She'd only worry herself to death.

Maynard tried desperately to envision himself living through the next half hour and hurried to stay on Cody's heels.

CHAPTER 12

Yellow lights lit up and began rotating at steady intervals along every corridor inside the base. Seconds later, the PA blared.

"Attention. Attention. A general quarantine has been issued due to a ..." The dispatcher searched for the appropriate words. "A level three quarantine lab has been breached. A virulent organism is at large. The infected individuals are in Corridor G moving together toward the cafeteria. Do not move in that direction. I repeat, do not move toward Corridor G. Recovery Team is en route to intercept and reestablish quarantine."

A siren whooped at two second intervals as Maynard and the Recovery Teams hurried toward the cafeteria. They hoped to arrive before the alien. It was dinner time. The cafeteria would be full. Easily a couple hundred people.

Maynard's heart raced, both from fear and exertion. When they arrived, he saw people moving, but without the appropriate level of urgency warranted by their current situation. Many were taking time to dump trays and toss them on the counter before leaving, like a bunch of robots stuck in their programming, shuffling along as death approached, swift and ravenous.

Then the sounds of muffled gunfire erupted from the hallway outside the east entrance. People stopped and cocked their heads, as if puzzling over whether it could actually be gunshots they were hearing above the din of the sounding alarm and wondering if, just possibly, the circumstances might require some immediate action on their part.

The east entrance doors flew open as two security guards half backpedaled, half stumbled into the cafeteria, guns pointed into the hallway, blazing. Two groups of thin tentacles shot into the room, sticking to both guards. An unseen force flexed and snatched the men through the air and into the body of the alien organism as it filled the doorway. Maynard and Cody watched as the guards were engulfed by the alien tissue and the creature squeezed through into the cafeteria, its dense, viscous mass unfurling until it stood above them all, head and shoulders reaching halfway to the second story vaulted ceiling.

"Holy shit," he muttered. "It's gotten bigger."

Of course, dumbass, he thought. *It's eaten more people, no doubt.*

Maynard gawked at the creature. Its head was a collection of human heads, their faces arrayed before him like petals on a flower. The mouths and respiratory tracts of the fallen had been preserved, however. Twelve of them roared in unison, tongues fully extended and quivering with fury and desire.

A wall of gunfire erupted from Cody and the rest of the unit, followed by Maynard. The four drones buzzed several feet above their heads firing small caliber munitions at the monster as well.

People shrieked astonished curses and fled in terror; like rats scurrying to jump ship, clambering to stuff themselves through one of only two exits left, and no one wanted to be last in line.

The alien's gelatinous structure absorbed the bullets. Some of the ballistic rounds splintered bones suspended in the organic strata on impact, but the shards were held relatively in place. Plasma rounds scorched the surface layer of the organism but inflicted no significant damage. Bryant's shotgun shells blew small, jagged holes in the alien's flesh but had no effect otherwise. The creature's exterior undulated back and forth in waves, wiping the injuries clean in seconds. Unfazed, it lurched toward the nearest people, large pseudopodia launching forward to snare and retrieve more food. More biomass.

The men with ballistic weapons ran dry, ejected magazines, and slapped new ones in. It was during this brief lull that Maynard heard the alien speak, saw the mouths of every head uttering guttural noises in chorus, attempting to form words without lips.

"Caaaahhhnnn ... Caahnn uuuunto neeeeee. Caahnn uuuuunto neeeee."

Its speech tapered off in a hiss each time before beginning again. Maynard's brain translated for him, though he truly wished it hadn't.

"Come … Come unto me," it kept saying, over and over.

"For fuck's sake, no," he said aloud. "God, no."

A cluster of tentacled limbs reached for the huddled, struggling masses.

A pleading gesture, almost, Maynard thought, right before they lashed out, snatching up the pink-skinned vermin in rapid succession. It reminded Maynard of his childhood. A plate of fresh baked cookies set down in front of him and his friends. A flurry of reaching limbs and fumbling fingers, and suddenly, all the cookies were gone. It was much the same now.

"Caaaahhhhnnnn …" he heard again.

"Burn this fucker, Stu!" Cody shouted.

Maynard saw one of the men with a flame unit sling his rifle, grab the nozzle from his back, and step forward. He pulled the trigger, and fire leapt onto the creature, all hunger and fury.

Twelve tongues flailed as twelve throats wailed in rage. The alien organism continued to absorb, digest, and reallocate its newly gained mass while it turned toward the man with the flame thrower.

"Back up, Stu!" Cody ordered the man. "You gotta keep your distance!"

Stu shuffled backwards in a hurry. The end of a tentacle snapped less than two feet away from his face and retracted.

"Fuck me," he shouted and kept backing up, faster now.

"Brandon," Cody called out. "Second flame unit up. You and Rooster flank left. Stu, you lay down a wall of flame between the workers and the creature. Rooster, eat the fucker's body up. Make it look worse than a teenage boy with acne. Hopefully, it will move our way."

The alien balked at the flames blocking its way and screeched as the tracer rounds riddled its flesh with hundreds of smoldering holes that filled in within seconds. Rooster, frustrated at the lack of lasting effect his weapon was having, started advancing on the thing. Stu screamed in his mic when he saw what Rooster was doing.

"Rooster! No! Back up, man! Back the fuck up! You're too close! You're too fucking close!"

No sooner than the words left Stu's mouth, numerous tentacles lashed out and wrapped around Rooster's body. They jerked with one huge spasm and sent his massive form flying into the creature's central body. He embedded head-first, up to his waist, in the cytoplasmic torso. The team watched as their partner was engulfed completely. They could see the man's suit twist and compact, face shield imploding as the torso cracked wide open like a coconut crushed beneath a rock. The creature dissected Rooster's bulky form, tearing portions of him from each area of the suit, then moving some parts along toward their new destination while others were digested and absorbed.

The drones flew forward, obeying Cody's kamikaze command. The fired a hail of small bullets, to no effect, but accelerated and smashed into the creature's body. Four drones, each carrying a pound of explosives on board for just such tactics, embedded themselves in the alien's bulk and detonated.

The gelatinous mass of the monster exploded into a bouquet of ragged, splayed protrusions, bowing and twisting like gnarled limbs on a dead tree while others arced back upon themselves, breaking waves of alien flesh wavering in the air for several seconds before the amalgam of man and alien parts began to coagulate and shift, moving back toward each other, until they merged and combined into their previous form.

The monster shook itself and roared then turned and all twelve faces assessed Cody and his men. It seemed to understand their tactic and appeared to decide it should acquire them first to limit their interference.

Its bulk was multiplying. The audible noises it made were near unbearable to Maynard. The twisting of joints in two, gristle separating from bone. The sounds of ripping flesh made him think of sharp scissors racing through thick fabric, and the relentless crunch of bones ending in hollow pops or sharp snaps made Maynard flinch.

Bodies of the fallen were twisted together like pieces of softened steel to reinforce the lower limbs. Dismembered arms and legs migrated into bulky bundles, stacked end to end, and a circle of outstretched hands adorning each appendage balled all their fingers into fists. The gigantic monstrosity planted these two new upper limbs on the floor and assumed a posture reminiscent of a gorilla displaying its dominance. The floor shook beneath them all on impact.

"Caaaahhhhnnnnn uuuuunto neeeeeeeee ..." the creature said and shook its twelve heads.

As it did, another thick stalk appeared on each shoulder, both swelling into bulging, bulbous pods. They quivered violently and burst open, each one blossoming into a circle of twelve heads. Its visage was beyond bizarre. Decapitated heads formed three sunflowers of meat and bone.

They sat like the three heads of Cerberus perched atop a grotesquely alien King Kong body, which sprouted tentacles and pseudopodia wherever necessary to help snatch more prey.

Maynard grew up on centuries-old literature and films and was familiar with their modern equivalents, which refused to die. The shadow of similarity with those mythological entities, as well as their basic mammalian counterparts, was clear, but never had he imagined anything as hideous, as perversely aberrant and heretical within the animal kingdom as what stood before them all now.

This *thing* violated the natural order with unbounded vigor and a supremely callous enterprise. Its will to expand was singular and unyielding. Its appetite, immeasurable. Inordinate annexation was both its nature and resolute aim. *No* was a foreign concept. Boundaries, limits, the individual—all were unrecognized by its merciless intellect.

It punched the ground with both fists, threw its three heads back, and trumpeted a thunderous bellow that rattled Maynard's chest and skull. Thirty-six tongues prophesied their pending annihilation through assimilation. Maynard, Cody, and the whole team slunk back at the primal display of power, terror rising in each one's gorge.

"Fuckin' hell," Cody said. "Run!"

They all fled in unchecked panic, and the thing pursued them. Only Brandon was left behind to bring up the rear and drive the creature forward with flames if necessary. Maynard ran fast as he could, but the HEVO suit and rifle made it difficult.

"Move your ass, Maynard!" Cody yelled over the mic from behind him. "Point that rifle at the ceiling with one hand and pump those elbows."

Behind Cody, Bryant hustled the best he could with the heavy weapon, while Stu paused to paint the corridor with fire as the creature contorted its frame, narrowing to slither through the tunnel, a thousand small pseudopodia gripping the walls to pull itself along.

Once in the corridor, it moved with blinding speed.

CHAPTER 13

"Griggs!" Cody shouted over the comms. "We're coming out the south entrance with our hair on fire and a bogey burning up our ass."

"Copy that, sir," Griggs responded and thumbed the safety off. He gritted his teeth and ground his boots into the rocky surface.

Moments later, the door opened, and Teams One and Two piled out at a sprint. Unlike the untrained workers in the cafeteria, they were disciplined enough to not jockey for position and slow the group down. Griggs saw orange flames flash and glow, illuminating the airlock as the interior door shut behind them. Cody dragged Stu outside and closed the outer door. They took off across the rocky terrain for the landing pad, a good two-hundred-meter sprint in full suit before them.

"Brandon," Cody called out over their comms. "Make sure that bastard follows us, then stand guard and make sure it doesn't try to get back in."

"Copy loud and clear, boss," Brandon said. "But I don't think there's going to be any problem getting it to follow you, though."

Cody and the others had only made it fifty meters when the outer airlock door blew off its tracks and tumbled across the planet's surface. The alien monstrosity exited, contorted and morphed, adapting its form to the open space. Once it stood at full height, the nightmarish colossus took off for them at a gallop, its movements awkward but far faster than Cody had anticipated.

Griggs squeezed the trigger and unleashed hell. A barrage of explosive shells impacted the gel-like medium, embedding themselves into it before exploding. The thing's amalgamated flesh warped and splayed, shrapnel burrowing paths through it that sealed up moments later. Nearby human components within were shredded, but overall, the grenades had little to no effect. The heads folded up like flower buds before they bloom, and the alien charged at Griggs. Despite his continued fire, the creature did not slow or deviate from its course.

"Get out of there, Griggs!" Cody shouted.

"Too late, boss man," he said with calm acceptance. "Fuck you, motherfucker!" he screamed and held the trigger down. Grenade after grenade launched into the thing but to no avail. He yelled long and loud as several small tentacles shot forward and wrapped around his HEVO suit, snatched him into the air, and proceeded to whip Griggs about, slamming him into the rocky surface over and over. His suit ruptured and split. The tentacles gripped and pried, opening his suit up like an octopus going after an oyster or clam. They pulled him out piece by piece while on the move, assimilating his mass and leaving the shattered suit behind.

"Stu, Bryant, Maynard," Cody yelled in sequence, "whatever you do, do *not* stop running for the ship. That's an order."

Cody dropped the rifle and pulled the large weapon off his back. He activated the tripod and set the plasma cannon in place. Every step the colossal creature took shook the ground and rattled the weapon, but Cody acquired his target and squeezed the trigger. A ball of green plasma energy discharged from the barrel and swelled in size to a meter in diameter. When it struck the creature, the thing roared silently in the vacuum of space. The tissue withered temporarily, leaving a sunken, smoldering crater.

Cody pulled the trigger rapid fire until it warned him of overheating and imminent shutdown. He looked back at the others. Stu was almost at the ship. Maynard and Bryant were a good fifty meters behind Stu. Cody paused to let the weapon cool off. It had slowed the alien down … some, but it was still closing the distance too fast. He squeezed off four more rounds before the gun auto-shutdown, then turned and ran for the ship.

"Don't wait for me," Cody told them over the comms. "When you get to the dropship, beeline for the airlock. I'll meet you there."

Maynard turned to look back. The thing was a good hundred meters away and recovering from the beating Cody gave it. Maynard told himself he'd make it. He might die from the run afterwards, but he'd make it.

Maynard clambered up the bay door ramp and turned around.

"Cody," he said. "Run faster. That thing is hauling ass."

Maynard could see Cody's helmet start to turn to try and look behind him and see where the thing was.

"Don't you look back, Cody!" Maynard yelled at him. "There's no time! Just run! Fucking run, man! Faster!"

The alien was devouring the distance with long bounding strides, charging towards Cody, hands and feet pounding the ground. Maynard couldn't help but note the similarity of the creature's stride to that of a gorilla rushing at an enemy was uncanny.

He's not going to make it, Maynard thought. *Fuck*.

"Don't look back, Cody," he said, fear causing his throat to constrict. "Don't look back."

At the change in Maynard's voice, Cody knew he was doomed. He pulled a grenade off his belt, yanked the pin, and turned around to face the thing bearing down on him. He might have imagined he would throw the grenade at the head of the creature, strike a vital blow or something.

But no such act would transpire. It trampled him a moment later. Mashed Cody's body into its own, sticking him within the alien organism. The grenade went off. It formed a small pocket in the alien's cytoplasm, allowing numerous pieces of shrapnel to punch their way through Cody's suit, killing him instantly. An easy out, comparatively.

Maynard gasped.

"What is it?" Stu asked over the comms.

"Cody's gone," he said and left it at that. "And that thing is coming hard."

Maynard turned and ran for the entrance to the airlock. He stood next to Stu, waiting until the alien knew where they were and committed to entering the ship.

It skidded to a stop, bent its three heads down, and opened them. It looked inside and seeing them there, began contorting itself to fit into the cargo bay. Maynard and Stu joined Bryant inside the airlock, shut the door, and shot the controls with a plasma rifle. They viewed the bay on a screen inset into the wall. When they saw the thing was entirely inside the cargo bay, they sealed it. The alien ignored the closing bay and continued to pursue them.

They opened the airlock to the outside and filed out. Closing the door behind them, they scrambled to get clear of the ship. Bryant ditched the belt-fed shotgun so he could run faster and caught up to Maynard.

"Wile-E?" Stu called out on comms. "You there?"

"Yes, sir!"

"Lift off, man!" Stu said. "Send this ugly motherfucker to space."

The ship's engine's fired, and it began its ascent.

The alien creature had underestimated the intelligence of its prey. The G-forces pulled against its mass as the ship blasted up into space above the exomoon. It raged through the dropship, forming limbs and tentacles to punch and slam against the inner walls of this flying metal trap it had been lured inside.

And then the alien stopped and considered … every ship has controls … and all it needed were the right codes to authorize access to the ship's systems … including navigation.

Codes it knew once resided in Rich Maloy's brain matter.

Codes it now possessed.

They all watched the dropship climb higher and higher, a blazing column of smoke and roiling flame trailing behind the ship as it made its way into orbit. As it drew near to passing by the station, something happened.

"What the fuck?" Wile-E said.

"What's wrong?" Hurley asked over the comms, waiting for the signal from Wile-E to blow the ship.

"I'm locked out," Wile-E said. "I'm fucking locked out. That thing has overridden my codes with Rich's. Has to be. Couldn't be anything else. The ship is altering course ... *it's turning around.*"

"You gotta be fucking kidding me," Maynard muttered.

"Blow it, Hurley!" Wile-E hollered. "Blow it, now, while it's still in orbit!"

"Copy that," Hurley acknowledged, and immediately pressed the detonator. A flash of reddish yellow light pulsed in the sky above the base. Maynard noticed it was dangerously close to the station.

"Done," Hurley declared.

Maynard's HUD flashed red as a request for video link popped up from Jenna. Maynard accepted the request and her face appeared.

"Maynard!" Jenna yelled. "What the hell just happened?"

"Are you okay?" he asked her. "Is the station damaged?"

"I'm fine," she replied, "and I think the station is okay. I haven't heard any hull breach alerts or anything like that. Now, *tell me* what the hell happened."

Her eyes demanded he spill the beans right away.

Dispatch called them on the radio right then.

"Dispatch to Recovery Team," Bill Reid said. "Do you copy?"

"Hold on, Jenna," Maynard hurried to say. "Dispatch is calling now." She started to say something, but he muted her and minimized the feed. He *had* to focus on whatever information was coming their way.

"Recovery Team here, I copy," Wile-E replied to dispatch. With Cody gone, he was next in command.

"I've got Commander Cranston from the station on the other line," dispatch advised. "I'm going to patch her through."

"Commander Cranston," Bill Reid said, "Recovery Team acting commander Wile-E is on the line. Go ahead."

"Station Commander Cranston, here," she said, making no attempt to hide the severe annoyance in her voice. "What *in the hell* is going on? A dropship just blew up off our port side. Our hull was peppered with debris before we could erect the blast shields. We're assessing damage now to see what kind of repairs we'll have to make ASAP."

Wile-E cocked his head and took a deep breath.

"Commander Cranston," Wile-E began, "you may have a hard time believing what I'm about to tell you, but I assure you, everything I'm about to say is absolutely true. I'm sure you're aware we unearthed an alien vessel down here. Subsequently, one of the miners, Maynard Creed, found a way inside the ship and located an egg like object. Project Manager Rich Maloy made the decision a few hours ago to crack the alien object open. What emerged was a highly intelligent alien organism whose aggressive nature is only matched by its voracious hunger. It managed to kill over fifty workers within the base in a very short time. The Recovery Team managed to lure it outside the base and into a dropship. Our plan was to send it into space and blow it up once it was well past the station. But once in orbit, the creature managed to override our controls and turned the dropship around to return to the planet surface. We couldn't allow that to happen and had to blow it immediately while it was still in orbit."

Commander Cranston's face flared red with incredulous anger at first, but she soon realized Wile-E was dead serious about everything he was saying. Anger visibly turned to concern as she listened intently to every word he spoke.

"Now," Wile-E continued, "what I say next is of the utmost importance, and you must do as I say, at once. Bring up all external video feeds for the last five minutes and begin scanning them. Conduct a scan outside the station for any sign of life as well. If the alien organism wasn't blown away from you into space, it very well could have been blown in your direction and be attached to the exterior of the station. If it is, I have no doubt that it will find a way to force itself inside. It knocked an airlock door completely off the track down here and sent it tumbling a good fifty meters across the planet's surface. This creature is immensely powerful and has grown to extraordinary proportions in a short time."

Her jaw dropped.

"How … how in the world did this thing grow so large in so short a time?" Cranston asked, then motioned to someone off screen and ordered them to start looking over the video feeds and scan for life signs outside the station. Wile-E waited for her to turn back and face the camera, then answered her question.

"This creature is some form of malleable alien tissue. It's viscous but firm, and whatever flesh it overtakes, it digests it, absorbs it somehow, and then redistributes the newly acquired biomass throughout its body to change its structure as it sees fit. Basically, its assimilating any and all biomass it can to grow itself into some freakish amalgam of both human and alien tissue. The more it eats, the bigger it gets."

Commander Cranston shook her head in disbelief.

"My god, that's nuts," she muttered and turned to the person off screen. "Anything yet?" she asked them.

"No, ma'am, not yet," the man responded, then a second later, he leaned in close to the screen.

"What the fuck?" Maynard heard the man say, a worried urgency leaping into the man's voice. "Boss! Come look at this?"

Cranston stepped out of the camera's view to take a close look at what her coworker had spotted.

"What the hell is that?" the man whispered.

Cranston scrutinized the paused video feed, trying to figure out just what she was looking at. It appeared to be multiple sections of distorted flesh that remained loosely attached to each other. It was suctioned to the exterior of her station amidst pieces of the dropship that had embedded in the hull.

"Holy shit," Cranston said. "Let it play."

The man hit play, and she watched as the alien creature reshaped its form into something ordered and terrifying, healing itself as it did so. Within half a minute, the torso was a solid piece riding on two huge legs and two long arms, like a gorilla, with three stalk-like necks protruding upward with large pods sprouting from the end of each one.

"God almighty, what the hell is that thing, sir?" Cranston asked Wile-E.

"Link me in on the video feed," Wile-E said, "but if it's what we just sent up there, your guess at what it is, is just as good as mine. We're flying in the dark here too."

The video link popped up on Wile-E, Hurley, Bryant, and Maynard's HUD. They watched the alien creature finish healing itself and begin traversing the station in search of a way in.

"Shut the hangar doors," Wile-E told Cranston. "Do it now."

Cranston relayed the order, and her crew member made it happen. A computer voice sounded in the background.

"Hangar bay exterior door has been compromised."

The whole station shuddered, and the image of Cranston vibrated on the screen.

"Oh fuck. Fucking Hell," Maynard blurted out.

CHAPTER 14

Even as all the creature's shredded pieces dispersed with the fragments of the dropship, the alien organism reached out, spreading its tissues to seek out its own to find them and bind them together, bring them all with it and not leave any disconnected from the whole.

But one globular mass full of shattered bone fragments escaped the organism's reach, its velocity and growing distance too much for either portion to make up as they stretched to reunite. For a microsecond, two tendrils of alien tissue extending toward one another, yearning to touch and bond, were within a handsbreadth of making contact, and then they were gone, moving in two different diametric directions, never to make contact again.

The creature's body shook with sorrow at the loss, a pang of agonizing finality lancing through every cell, the intellect within each one crying out for their divided kin, sundered and isolated, beyond reach.

The alien organism was not accustomed to the pain of *forced* separation, and never before had that separation been permanent. The sensation of this new reality filled it with heretofore unexperienced indignation. A vindictive furor smoldered in every cell of its being as it watched the station grow closer.

Huge clumps of its biomass slammed against the exterior of the orbital station along with all its other pieces, both large and small, all of them, except the lost mass, connected to one another by a veritable network of thin strings of tissue. They stuck to the hull of the station, clinging together as the alien drew its tissues toward a central location, consolidating itself once again.

In moments, it formed itself into a roiling wave-like mass and moved toward a destination it pulled from the brains of Rich Maloy and others. A hangar bay. An airlock. A way into the station where more soft skin organisms awaited. Not the ones responsible for its current grief, but it would vent its fury on them nonetheless.

They watched the video feed, which was now behind real time where the man had rewound it.

"Fast forward the feed," Cranston told the man off camera.

"Hull Breach on Deck D in the hangar bay," the computer voice informed them. "Interior airlock door has been compromised. Sealing off Hallway D."

"Oh god," Maynard said. "It's inside the station. It's gotta be inside the station. You all need to hide. Get as far away from the hangar bay as possible and hide."

The video link caught up to real time, showing the alien creature wreck the exterior bay door to the hangar and slither inside, where it proceeded to rip both airlock doors from their housings and make its way inside the station.

"Oh my god," said Cranston. "It's inside the station ... and we have no way out now."

"Maynard is right," Wile-E cut in. "All of you need to run and hide and stay clear of that creature until help can arrive."

"And when might that be?" she asked, a dreadful look invading her countenance.

"I don't know," Wile-E said. "Maynard. You got any idea?"

"Well," Maynard said, "if corporate retasked the nearest super freighter to detour here and pick up our derelict spaceship like we asked, it should be here in about six months. If not, it's going to be a year from now, easily, before we receive any outside help."

Maynard watched Cranston's face fall.

"You're fucking serious?" she asked, her temper rising in an instant. "If that creature is as nasty as you describe," Cranston said, "we won't last six weeks, much less six months to a year. Sounds like you inadvertently delivered us a death sentence."

"I'm sorry, Commander Cranston," Wile-E said. "I'm afraid you're right. We didn't intend for it to reach the station, but we didn't have much choice either. We *had* to blow the ship when we did."

Cranston wiped her face with both hands, then stood erect, fixed her eyes on the camera, and tried to burn her gaze into Wile-E's soul through the video feed.

"This ... this is not acceptable. You are the Recovery Team. Come recover. Fly a fucking ship up here and save my people. Do your job."

Wile-E felt a searing thrust of guilt pierce his heart and looked away from Cranston.

She was right. They were the Recovery Team. But if he flew a ship up there to rescue as many crew as possible, it wouldn't be his ass on the line. He'd be safely inside the dropship waiting to fly them back down to the surface. The rest of the team would be the ones risking their lives going near that alien monster again. Wile-E couldn't imagine ordering them to do that. None of them were trained for this. None of them signed up for something like this. It was a nightmare sprung to life. An impossible, completely unforeseeable scenario.

"Okay," he said and turned his eyes back to the camera to meet Cranston's. "Here's the facts, and we'll go from there. First, we only have one dropship left, with a capacity of maybe ten to fifteen people in HEVO suits, which you're going to need to reach the ship by spacewalk. So limited space means everyone can't be saved at once. Which means we'll have to leave some people behind on the station with the creature while we shuttle the first round of survivors down to the base. You're going to have to decide who goes on the first run, not me. Second, I am not ordering my men to go on this suicidal mission. This is outside our training, not even remotely in our swim lane of things we've prepared for or that our job description spells out as a duty. So, it's volunteers only. No volunteers, no mission."

Wile-E paused, and Maynard cut in.

"I volunteer, sir," Maynard said loudly, making sure he was heard. "But only if Jenna Parks is in the first group of survivors to be brought down."

Maynard spoke his piece and stood silent, waiting for a response.

"I can't guarantee that," Cranston said.

"Yes, you can," Wile-E countered. "Maynard may be motivated by love, but Jenna Parks is the chief doctor up there and a high value asset to our mission. You *will* prioritize her in the first group. That's an order. Deal?"

Cranston appeared frustrated but nodded her head in agreement.

"Deal … if we have a rescue mission," she said. "Any other volunteers? Or is the miner the only one with balls of steel?"

Wile-E cracked a half smile at her challenge.

"Well, boys," he said to his team. "Who's up for rescuing some juicy colonists from a raging alien monstrosity? I'm in, and Maynard's in. Any other takers?" He paused, then spoke again. "If you're worried about missing happy hour, don't be. It won't take long. We'll either be back here within a few hours or dead and you won't care anyway. So, who's in? I need two more people."

"I'm in," said Hurley.

"Me too," said Bryant.

"Excellent," Wile-E said. "We've got a party date, boys. Let's put it in high gear and get prepped for launch ASAP." Wile-E turned his attention back to Cranston. "Stay safe, and we'll be in touch to coordinate a rendezvous point with you once we're in the air."

Cranston nodded silently.

"Recovery Team out," Wile-E said and cut the feed.

CHAPTER 15

Maynard unmuted Jenna and enlarged the video feed. Her eyes smoldered with anger.

"Jenna? Can you hear me?"

"Yes!" she answered. "*Now* I can! What the hell did you mute me for?"

"I had to hear dispatch and the info we were receiving. The Recovery Team and Commander Cranston on the station were exchanging details."

"Details about what?" Jenna cut in. "Just what the hell is going on, May? They're saying a dropship blew up outside the station and now the hangar and its airlock are compromised. They're closing off every entry to the hangar along with every corridor that connects to it."

"I know, Jen," he said. "I know. Let me explain. It's complicated."

Jenna's head pulled back, chin down, eyebrows bunched in a deep furrow.

"What the fuck did y'all do?" she asked, fear and anger lacing her voice.

"I found something in that alien ship. Turned out it was an egg of sorts. Rich cracked it open. The thing came out and devoured him, absorbed him. Then it got loose and started eating everyone it came across. Damn thing gets bigger and bigger with everything it eats. It's an amalgam of sorts. A cytoplasmic aggregate of everything it consumes. It absorbs and reallocates the biomass it acquires into whatever form it sees fit to use. And so far, those forms have been fucking terrifying. The motherfucker is hungry too. Like, *seriously* fucking hungry."

Jenna's face contorted through a series of expressions. Disbelief, acceptance, horror, and, finally, fury. Maynard recognized her progression and quickly tried to divert responsibility away from himself. It hadn't been his call, anyway.

"Look, it wasn't my call to release this thing like a moron, and we didn't intend to blow the ship up next to the station. That wasn't the plan."

"Well, genius," Jenna fired back, "what *was* the plan?"

"Well," Maynard explained, "when the head of the Recovery Team, Cody … when he realized we couldn't stop the creature, he decided to trap it in the drop ship, send it out into space, and blow it up with a payload of explosives on board. And everything was going according to plan. We trapped it, we launched it into space, and it was flying past the station when the damned thing managed to override the controls and started turning the ship around to return to the base. We couldn't let that happen. There are way more colonists down here than up there. We had to blow the dropship while it was still in orbit and the pieces and the monster wouldn't just plummet to the surface. It was a risk we had to take. Unfortunately, it was close enough that the explosion allowed the creature to attach itself to the station and now it's forced its way inside."

"And where is this Cody fucker now?" Jenna asked, her anger blazing hot.

"He's dead, Jenna," Maynard said, blunt and matter of fact, but with a distinct tone of mourning in his voice. "He died to save the rest of the team, so we could complete the mission."

Jenna was quiet, the oxygen fueling her fire snatched away.

"How soon can we expect help?" she asked.

"Well, if we had to wait on HQ, it would be about six months, most likely," Maynard said.

"Six months?" Jenna half shouted. "Are you fucking kidding me? Is that the best they can do?"

"As a matter of fact," Maynard said, "it is. If they don't retask the nearest super freighter, it'll be a year before a ship gets here."

"Maynard," Jenna complained, "it sounds like even a few days is too long to be locked in here with that thing you described. We're all going to die, aren't we?" Jenna looked more pissed off than sorrowful at the revelation.

"No," he advised her, "because we're going to fly a dropship up there and save as many as we can."

"But you can't fit that many in a dropship bay, can you?" Jenna asked.

"Well, no, not a huge amount. Around ten to fifteen people wearing HEVO suits can fit inside the bay, but you're going to be in the first group we bring back down. It was my sole condition for volunteering to go on this mission."

Jenna's heart melted. She sighed and pressed a hand against her chest.

"Are you serious, May?" she asked. "You're coming up here to get me with this killer alien on the loose?"

"You bet your fine ass I am," he said and winked. "Now, listen to me, it's crucial you do what I say. Get as far away from the hangar as possible. Get yourself a HEVO suit and hide out somewhere we can reach you. Preferably, somewhere near an airlock. That would probably make for the easiest extraction. Also, stay in contact with Commander Cranston. She should be designating who comprises the first group. So, coordinate with her and have the others meet you wherever you're hiding out at. And remember: everyone needs a HEVO suit. Y'all are going to have to spacewalk to reach the dropship. Okay?"

"Okay," she said, "but I've never spacewalked before. I doubt if any of us here have ever done it other than Maintenance. Have you?"

"Yeah," Maynard said. "I've done it a few times. I'll be fine. And so will you. I'm sure we'll anchor a cable from ship to station so all you have to do is hook onto it and fire your thrusters. It'll take you straight to the dropship. No fuss, no muss, so don't fret over it. Bottom line, one way or another, I'm coming to get you. You hear me? I'm coming to get you as soon as we can prep and launch. You stay safe. Stay hidden. And lock every door possible. Keep us linked so we can communicate at any time. Okay?"

"Okay," Jenna said. She was smiling and crying at the same time. "Will do."

"I love you, Jen, and I'm sorry things went sideways. Hang in there, and I'll see you as soon as I can get up there."

"I love you too," she said for the first time. It was the first time for them both. Maynard smiled, his heart warming at her words.

"Okay," he said, "I have to go. Gotta help check on the wounded here and then help prep for take-off. Message me with your location and coordinates when you find a hiding spot. Talk to you soon"

They blew each other kisses and minimized the video feed.

"So, you sure you're up to this?" Wile-E asked Maynard.

Maynard looked the former soldier in the eye.

"Yeah. I've done mining in Zero-G, with tethers and magnetic boots. I'll be fine with the spacewalk, and I can help the survivors get hooked in and across to the ship."

"All right," Wile-E said. "All right. I guess you are good for it. But what about inside? You're not that proficient with weapons, and Cody won't be there for you to stick to like glue. Might be best if you stay outside while Bryant and Hurley go inside to retrieve them."

Maynard nodded in agreement.

"You may be right. And if everything is looking squared away, I'm fine with that arrangement. But that's my fucking girl up there. The love of my life. If shit goes sideways, I'm going in to help. Okay?"

Wile-E shrugged his shoulders, not entirely confident, but at this point, not entirely committed to an opposing viewpoint either.

"Okay, Maynard," he said. "Deal. Now, let's get inside and see if anyone needs help, then we'll pull up some specs on the station's design and layout and figure out our approach."

Maynard nodded and joined Wile-E, Stu, Bryant, and Hurley as they made their way back to the base. The southern airlock was demolished, so they headed for the southeast airlock instead. When they arrived, Brandon was waiting for them.

After they transitioned through the airlock and into the base itself, they all took their helmets off. Maynard looked at Brandon.

"What's the status in here, man? Do the medics need help treating the wounded?"

"Wounded?" Brandon asked, his face scrunching up in puzzlement. "There aren't any wounded. If that thing touched them, it took them, and there was no escaping it. Hell, there's hardly even any blood in the cafeteria. That fucker slurped it up as it moved across the room. All it leaves behind is inorganic stuff. Clothing. HEVO suits. Jewelry. Shit like that. If it can eat it, there won't be a trace. C'mon. Follow me."

Maynard walked after the man, and the others fell in behind him, but they didn't need Brandon to lead the way. They followed the trail of discarded clothing items, gawking at the sheer number of people they represented. The cafeteria was far worse. More clothes were scattered about there, with a particularly large deposit in the middle of the room along with Rooster's mauled HEVO suit. Rings and necklaces were visible as well on the floor, but there was no blood anywhere. Maynard didn't see a drop, just the cast aside items that once clothed and adorned more colonists than he could presently calculate.

Maynard was in shock for a long moment at the realization. Nothing they'd ever seen before could compare. It was surreal … unreal … beyond the imagination and immeasurably more terrifying than anything he'd ever experienced before in his life. He shook his head and wiped his face.

"Reset, May," he told himself. "Get it together. Focus on the job, not the horrific details."

His mind fumbled for what they needed to do next before acquiring the drop ship and preparing the rescue mission. He turned to Wile-E.

"We need to send a transmission to corporate HQ on Earth, ASAP, and notify them of what has happened."

"Agreed," Wile-E said. "Let's head to Dispatch and do that first. Afterwards, we'll start prepping another dropship and figuring out how we're going to execute this rescue mission."

CHAPTER 16

"Calvin," Commander Cranston said to her tech specialist, "give me live video feed of that alien creature. I want to know where it is every second.

"Kaileigh," Commander Cranston said, turning to address her communications officer, "put the station on red alert, sound the alarms, and make an announcement that a hostile and exceptionally large alien lifeform has made entry to our station via the hangar airlock. They need to find a place to hide, preferably someplace they can seal off and secure. Lock their doors and remain quiet. Advise them a Recovery Team will be inbound from the surface ASAP."

"Yes, ma'am," Kaileigh replied, then did as instructed. A Klaxon alarm blared, and yellow lights activated along every hall, rotating in their housings. After five cycles, Kaileigh turned them off and spoke.

"Alert," she said. "All crew and colony workers currently onboard. This is *not* a drill. I repeat, this is *not* a drill. We are now at red alert status. The station has been compromised and boarded by a hostile alien life form discovered on the exomoon. It is large, it is hungry, and it is extremely aggressive. Hide. Now. Someplace you can secure yourself inside, preferably. Remain quiet. Remain still. A Recovery Team will be inbound from the exomoon's surface ASAP. Directions will be announced as far as where to go when they arrive to evacuate the station. Bridge out."

"Commander?" Calvin said, urgency filling his voice.

"Yes, Calvin," Cranston answered. "What is it?"

"The creature is moving at alarming speed. It's entered the airducts and is spreading upward through the station."

"Show me," she said.

Calvin cast the video feed to the large screen above his workstation. They watched as the alien amalgam rushed through a corridor, drove its substantial mass into an airduct, then popped out on another level, swarmed down a hallway, snatching people up who happened to be seeking somewhere to hide, absorbing them, then crashing into another airduct and disappearing off the screen.

"Oh my god," Calvin said.

"What?" Cranston barked.

"It appears to be making a beeline toward the bridge," he said.

"All right," Cranston shouted. "All of you! Evacuate the bridge now. Get to the elevator and disperse to a lower level."

They all stared at her wide eyed.

"But isn't it safer here?" Kaileigh asked.

Cranston stared at the girl.

"No!" she yelled at the communications officer. "It is not! This creature is intelligent. It knows the bridge is the point of command and control of the vessel. That's probably why it's coming here first. Now, move your asses!"

Cranston wasn't sure if what she just said was true or not, but it sounded good. What she really hoped was that them fleeing would distract the creature, that it would go after the fleeing targets in its path while she sent a message to Songbird and attempted to secure herself in her office.

Fuck them, she thought.

She shut the bridge door and sealed it with her authorization code, then ran into her office and did the same. She pulled the thin cord from her implant and plugged into the computer. She initiated the encrypted communications app. Their level shuddered as the alien burst out of an airduct into a room, then emerged into the hallway leading to the bridge. Cranston felt it, but shut off within her office, she did not hear the screams of the people who served under her as the alien's tentacles snatched them up and incorporated them into its mass.

"Begin message," Cranston said. "Songbird. This is Blue Falcon. I need immediate emergency evacuation."

The door to the bridge buckled with a resounding BOOM as the alien's mass slammed into it.

"What the fuck?" Cranston said as she braced out to stabilize herself, then continued her message. "A hostile alien organism from the ship on the exomoon is loose on the station and its killing everyone. I repeat—"

BOOM!

The alien struck the bridge door again, and this time, both sections folded outward, wrapping around to touch the wall on each side.

"Oh my god!" Cranston yelped then continued in a whisper. "I repeat. I require immediate emergency evacuation. Please, Songbird. Send help now."

Her office door opened, and she only had time enough to think who could override her authorization codes. And then she realized, Rich could, right before the alien organism swarmed into the room and flowed over her body, enveloping her and beginning the assimilation process.

The creature left her head exposed outside its body. Cranston screamed when her flesh dissolved, then wailed in agony as her bones snapped and joints folded in unnatural directions or twisted free of their moorings, connective tissues snapping. At last, her spine stretched, elongating until a loud crack announced the removal of her head.

The alien prodded at her skull on one side, and discovering some form of embedded technology, decided to retain it after accessing Commander Cranston's brain. It utilized an undigested crew member's hand along with Cranston's memories and authorization codes to lock the bridge doors and access the computer system. It shut down the alert and compartmentalized access to security and other critical systems to the bridge, with only Commander Cranston's or Rich Maloy's codes allowing access. Afterwards, it rose up and entered the air ducts above Cranston's former desk and rushed off to another level in search of more sustenance.

CHAPTER 17

The Klaxon alarm blared, but the man on top of the Sex Synth, determined to finish, did not stop thrusting. Savannah listened as the alarm cycled five times and stopped.

"Alert," she heard crew member Kaileigh announce. "All crew and colony workers currently onboard. This is *not* a drill. I repeat, this is *not* a drill. We are now at red alert status. The station has been compromised and boarded by a hostile alien life form discovered on the exomoon. It is large, it is hungry, and it is extremely aggressive. Hide. Now. Someplace you can secure yourself inside, preferably. Remain quiet. Remain still. A Recovery Team will be inbound from the exomoon's surface ASAP. Directions will be announced as far as where to go when they arrive to evacuate the station. Bridge out."

Savannah looked at the man as he locked out his hips, whole body tensed, eyes closed.

"I believe this is not a drill. You should get dressed and seek shelter."

The man finally opened his eyes and stared at Savannah. He looked confused.

"What?" he asked.

"Didn't you hear, hon?" Savannah asked. "Some kind of alien organism is onboard. Something they found on the moon … and its dangerous."

"A fucking alien? Are you serious?"

"Well, sugah," Savannah said, "apparently, the bridge is. They said, 'This is not a drill'."

The man gave her a droll look, then stood and slid his clothes on.

"Okay then, honey," the man said in a sarcastic tone, "since I'm leaving mid-way through our scheduled time, I'm only paying half the credits."

"That is a reasonable proposition," Savannah said, then a moment later. "Refunded."

"Awesome," the man said, then grabbed his ID and cred stick "Let yourself out. I'm gonna see what the hell is happening out there."

"Sure thing," Savannah said.

The man headed for the door. As it opened, Savannah heard the pounding feet of people running away from the bridge and saw them pass by the door. The man stepped into the hallway and looked down toward the elevator where they appeared to be heading. He startled and bolted toward the bridge. Savannah watched as some of the people who had just run by were now passing her door again and heading back to the bridge, except now they were all screaming, quite loudly even.

Seconds later, a gigantic mass of amorphous, red-tinted, transparent organic material moved past her door as well, filling the hallway. She saw bodies trapped inside its form in various stages of what appeared to her at a glance to be digestion. Her facial recognition software picked up on one face, identifying it as the comms officer, Kayleigh Renalto, whom she had just heard minutes before over the station broadcast system.

Her dormant systems kicked in at the sight of crew members being injured and possibly terminated. Combat tactical analysis came online first and spun up after several seconds. Her door timed out and shut automatically.

"Evaluating," she said out loud to no one. A minute later, she walked to the door, opened it, and exited the man's room into the hallway, her pink camisole and matching undergarments fluttering gently as she moved.

Savannah looked around. She saw piles of clothing laying on the floor of the hallway, spread out along the length of it. The bridge door appeared intact and was shut. No human was in sight. Savannah walked to the bridge door and checked to see if it would open.

It would not.

She checked each room along the hallway as she moved toward the elevator. Some of them were open. Those that were not, she forced open. None of them were occupied. Her dormant subsystems attempted to link with the bridge to confer with command and determine if any humans were indeed in imminent danger. When no contact could be made, her subsystems reached a conclusion.

"Unable to link with command," she spoke aloud. "No humans in danger detected. Protocols satisfied. Return to Regeneration Station and standby for further instructions from command."

Savannah tried to call the elevator but received no response. She proceeded to the emergency stairwell and walked down one level. There, she exited onto the hallway and proceeded to her quarters, into her bedroom, and beyond into the bathroom where her Regeneration Station was located. She stepped forward, turned around, and backed up until her spine touched the wireless charging network and connected with the nanobot delivery system. There, Savannah powered down into sleep mode, awaiting a human presence or further instructions.

CHAPTER 18

"Bill," Wile-E said to the dispatcher, "I need Hyper Light Comms online ASAP. Tight beam laser encrypted transmission to HQ on Earth. It's going to be a Code Red SOS."

"Understood, sir," Bill replied. "Standby while I establish a link with the orbital comms array."

Seconds ticked by and Wile-E and Maynard both anxiously waited for Bill to establish the link.

"Link established," Bill updated them. "Locking Transmitter Dish on target … coordinates uploaded. Tracking …. Tracking … on target … aaaannnnd target lock established. Sir, you may begin recording your message in three, two, one."

Bill pointed a finger at Wile-E.

"This is a Code Red SOS," Wile-E began. "I repeat, this is a Code Red SOS. We have a Category Five Unchecked Echo-Tango Incursion. I repeat a Category Five Unchecked Echo-Tango Incursion. I am William Ellison, ranking officer of the surviving members of the Recovery Team. An entrance to the alien vessel was located and a portion of the interior was investigated. An item which looked similar to an oversized petrified egg was discovered. Base manager, Rich Maloy, conducted x-rays and resonance scans on the item. Afterwards, he decided to drill into it. He released an alien organism that is incredibly hostile and hungry. It absorbs human biomass to increase its own size. Recovery Team tried to stop it, but our weapons were completely ineffective. We trapped it on a drop ship and sent it up into space, where we detonated a small payload of explosives inside the craft. Unfortunately, it was unharmed and managed to reach the station and make entry. Cody Wilson, former leader of Recovery Team was killed in the process of trapping the alien creature in the drop ship. We're going to try and rescue as many people from the station as possible before the creature hunts them all down. No one, I repeat, no one should attempt to board the station. I suggest we implement a general quarantine. Please advise what further action you wish us to take while awaiting arrival of the evac ship and when we can expect it. Wile-E out."

He ended the recording, and the Dispatcher sent the message.

"How long before we can expect a reply?" Wile-E asked the Dispatcher.

"I sent it as a high priority tight beam communication," the man said. "A couple hours, most likely."

"Notify me as soon as you get something."

"Will do, sir."

"All right, Maynard," Wile-E said, "let's get back to our ready room and draw up a plan."

An hour later, Wile-E and Maynard stood around a projection screen, scanning through the station schematics.

"I only see two options," Wile-E concluded. "Either we spacewalk to the trash chute entrance and walk inside from there or we spacewalk to the base of the communication's array and enter the airlock at that location. If I have to choose, I'd take the airlock, but it all depends on what your girl's able to reach. Hit her up on comms. See what she can tell you, and we'll go from there."

Maynard nodded in agreement, then went over to a computer and opened a link and sent Jenna a video request. She didn't answer. He waited until it timed out and tried again. And again.

"That's not good," Bryant said, oblivious to the callous nature of his comment. Wile-E cut a look his way, but Bryant just shrugged his shoulders and raised his hands palm up.

A cold sweat broke out on Maynard's forehead, and he suddenly felt nauseated. He closed his eyes and swallowed.

"C'mon, Jenna," he mumbled under his breath and hit send again. Each chirping tone gnawed at Maynard's heart while he waited. Just before it timed out once more, the link opened, and Jenna's face filled the screen. Maynard could see metal moving by her at the outer edges of the video. A loud klaxon-like siren was blaring in the background. Maynard sat upright and leaned toward the screen.

"What's going on, Jenna?" he asked. "Where are you?"

Jenna looked up, away from the screen, glanced down at Maynard for a second, and looked away again.

"I'm running for my god damned life, just like everyone else up here is doing right now."

"What the hell?" Maynard exclaimed. "That thing has already escaped the hangar area?"

"Yes!" she yelled. "It got out of there within a few minutes after we talked. Apparently, Commander Cranston didn't have sufficient authority to override whatever code that fucking thing managed to enter. Before we knew it, the creature was squeezing itself through the hallways and headed for the bridge."

"Holy shit," Maynard muttered, smearing the palm of one hand from forehead to mouth and pinching his fingers around his lips. "It's got Rich Maloy's codes. They trump everything on this god damn project, colony or station."

"Great," Jenna yelled. "Well, this whole rescue mission plan you mentioned. Got an update on when that might happen? Not sure how long I've got."

"Uh, yeah," Maynard said, trying to shake the shock off. "We've figured out two possible locations we can enter at. So, it really depends on what you're most able to reach."

"Okay," Jenna said. "Give a girl some options and let's see what I can do."

"Well, the preferred option would be the airlock at the base of the communications array. But if that isn't feasible, then the trash chute is plan B."

"Communications array airlock," Jenna said. "I can make it there for sure. Not sure how many people will make it there with me, though. People are running like roaches when the lights come on. How many people did you say you can you fit on the drop ship, again?"

"Ten to fifteen," Maynard said.

"Can you be a bit more specific?" she asked. "I'd hate to have to tell five people sorry, too bad when that thing is breathing down our necks."

Maynard turned to look at Wile-E. "What do you think?"

Wile-E came over to the computer screen.

"Jenna, this is Wile-E. I'm the guy who will be piloting the dropship. If I were going to be realistic, I'd say we can definitely fit an additional twelve people in full HEVO suits into the dropship bay. But, don't forget, that means anyone you bring along also *has to have* a HEVO suit. No suit, no spacewalk to our dropship."

There was a silent pause before Jenna answered.

"Gotcha. I know there's a few suits at the airlock by the communications array, but besides that, I have no idea. If I can gather some others, it won't be more than three or four of them, I suspect. Shit's gone crazy in here. What's your expected ETA?"

Wile-E rubbed his chin.

"I'd say an hour and a half prep time, thirty minutes flight time, and maybe ten minutes at most to spacewalk to your location and connect a tether line back to the ship for everyone to hook to. So, get to the airlock and suit up. When we contact you, put the helmets on and be prepared to go as soon as we knock on the door. Copy?"

Jenna nodded her head.

"I copy," she acknowledged. "Maynard," she said, looking at the video screen of her wrist mounted comms unit.

"Yeah," he answered.

"Don't leave a girl hangin', ya hear?"

She blew him a kiss and closed the video link.

Wile-E tried to open a link to Commander Cranston and see what her status was. After five tries, he gave up and assumed the worst.

CHAPTER 19

Maynard, Wile-E, Bryant, and Hurley made all preparations with due haste. Stu and Brandon assisted them, but they would be staying behind so they could maximize the number of survivors they could fit in the dropship bay.

Maynard accompanied Hurley and Bryant to the weapon's locker to change their load out.

"Energy weapons and normal ballistic rounds didn't do shit to that that thing earlier," Bryant said. "Only the flamers did," he continued, "but we can only carry so much fuel, and if we end up engaging it outside the station, flamers won't be any use in space."

"So, what are we going to use?" Maynard asked, not hiding his concern.

"I think our best option," Hurley spoke up, "is to supplement the flame units with white phosphorus shotgun shells and grenades."

Bryant grinned big as he spoke. "You read my mind, Hurley."

"What's white phosphorus?" Maynard asked.

"The fingertips of hell," Bryant said. "They burn the fuck out of whatever they touch, and they don't stop burning for a long time. We've got grenades that explode with white phosphorus shrapnel, and we have smaller shotgun shells that contain white phosphorus. They don't penetrate as deep as normal shot on impact, but they will burn a path inside like a rat on fire trying to eat his way through your guts to get away."

"Lord have mercy," Maynard said. "That sounds inhumane."

"Maybe so," Hurley said, "but you can't argue with their combat effectiveness. Burning flesh has a way of rearranging any man's priorities. Hard to focus on fighting when all you want to do is make the fire go out."

"So," Bryant spoke up as he reached inside a locker. "Flame units for Hurley and I. Maynard, you will be carrying a Pumpkin Puncher with white phosphorus shells." Bryant handed Maynard a large combat class shotgun. "Hurley will have one as a backup too, plus his shield. This version," Bryant said and indicated the gun Maynard was now holding, "utilizes large magazines. With the smaller two inch white phosphorus shells, you can carry thirty shells per magazine. Now, me," he said as he pulled another weapon from the locker, "I'll be toting the 'Fuck You and Everyone Near You' model. Same basic shotgun but belt fed, and the standard shells are typically four and a half inches long instead of three and a half. Lot more shot flying downrange." Bryant smiled big. "For fighting this alien thing, though, I'll have several hundred rounds of the same white phosphorus shells mounted to the back of my suit beside the shotgun rack, so I'll have to carry the flame unit separately."

"And I'll have a flamer unit with the fuel tank attached to the back of my suit," said Hurley. "I can carry more fuel that way. Maynard, you'll carry two of that shotgun model. One on your back as a spare in addition to your primary weapon."

Maynard nodded. Hurley hefted the weapon and demonstrated its use, how to shoulder it properly and control recoil, then pointed out the selector switch.

"This switch here," Hurley said, "is to select the form of firing you prefer. Down is semi-auto. Pull the trigger once and you get one shot. Horizontal is three-shot bursts. Pull the trigger once and three shots fire off automatically. And up is full auto. Just hold the trigger down, and it will dump the whole magazine. And lastly, if something malfunctions on you," Hurley instructed, "and the creature is closing in, don't waste time trying to fix it. Just drop it and draw your backup. Copy?"

Maynard nodded again. "Copy," he said.

They began outfitting their suits and arming themselves with everything they would need.

"What about drones?" Maynard asked Hurley. He knew the station's hallways were too small for the battle armor, but some drones might be useful, he thought. "Can we use them?"

Hurley shook his head.

"Unfortunately, no," he answered. "Cody was the only one with the hardware necessary to fully control them effectively in the middle of battle."

Maynard nodded in understanding and went back to loading spare magazines for the shotguns.

Just before they were ready to secure the weapons locker and leave, Bryant picked up a belt of white phosphorus grenades.

"Can't forget these babies," he said with an impish smile and chuckle.

An hour and twenty-two minutes after Maynard ended his video link with Jenna, they were on the dropship and ready to launch. As they were all buckling in, Dispatch called.

"Dispatch to Wile-E."

"Wile-E here," he answered. "Go ahead with your traffic, Dispatch."

"HQ responded."

"What did they advise?" Wile-E inquired.

"HQ advises that the nearest super freighter, the Queen Antares, has been retasked to arrive at our location in six months," Dispatch said. "They've instructed us to order the colony to continue with normal mining operations until the Queen Antares arrives. 'Keeping busy will be good for the workers while they wait,' it says."

"Hmmph," Wile-E said. "I doubt they give a god damn about the workers. They just don't want us to lose our shit and destroy this place. Would cut into their profit margins."

"Much as I hate to admit it," Maynard spoke into his helmet mic, "they're probably right under these circumstances."

"Probably," Wile-E said, then responded to Dispatch. "We copy you, Dispatch. Send a reply that we received the communication and will comply. Recovery Team out. Counting down to launch."

Wile-E flipped the final switches and began the countdown to lift off. Thruster rockets ignited and roared in Maynard's ears, vibrating his entire body. His head bobbled inside the HEVO helmet. His teeth chattered, and he clamped his jaw shut.

"What's wrong, Maynard?" Bryant asked mockingly. "This is the best part."

Maynard glanced at the man's grinning face looking out from his helmet visor, then looked away, closed his eyes, and pressed the back of his helmet into the headrest. Maynard hated this part, but he *really* hated the next stage.

The second afterburner kicked in and lift off turned into a rapid take off. The G forces pinned Maynard back in his seat and plastered his back against the inside of his suit. He actually thought his stomach might touch his spine. He got lightheaded, and for a few seconds, the edges of his vision began to grow black and narrow. His head swooned.

"WOOOOOOOOOOOOOOOOOOOOO!!!" Bryant screamed across from him like a kid on a rollercoaster.

Breathe, you dumbass, Maynard reminded himself and forced his body to blow out hard, then suck air in and repeat. Seconds ticked by as Maynard silently counted off the breathing sequence. *IN one-two-three-four, HOLD one-two-three-four, OUT one-two-three-four.* Three times he did this, and then the secondary thrusters cut out. A short time later, he felt the buoyancy of zero-G kick in, and Wile-E started applying reverse thrusters to check their closing speed, slowing them so he could maneuver into position near the communication array's airlock.

Maynard detected a beeping noise. Opening his eyes, he saw a blinking red light in the corner of his HUD. It had to be Jenna.

"Open video link," he said, and the window popped up.

"May-nard!" Jenna hollered.

"Jenna!" he cried out, trying to lean forward in his seat unsuccessfully. "What's wrong?"

"This creature is relentless, merciless." She breathed hard, her movements shaky and frantic as she ran, holding the wrist screen toward her face. "It's killed so many. I don't know if anyone else is left besides me and the small group of people I've picked up along the way. It diverted to the bridge for a bit, but it's been on a seek and destroy … or seek and consume mission ever since. It spread itself throughout the ventilation shafts and ducts and snatched up a lot of people who were fleeing in different directions. I thought we lost it after it took several of the people I was moving with and left, but I don't think so now. I can hear it moving through the ship toward our location. I hope y'all are almost here, because we're not too far from the airlock. ETA ten minutes. Tops."

"Yes," Maynard half yelled. "We're almost in position."

"Good thing," she said, "but you're sure as hell cutting this close."

"What do you mean?" Bryant cut in on Maynard's comms, his voice inside Maynard's helmet. "We're eight minutes early."

"What was that?" Jenna asked.

"Don't worry about it," Maynard assured her. "We're almost there."

There was a loud explosion somewhere near Jenna's location. It shook the station, and her camera feed jostled about. The video link window filled with static and wavy lines, but Maynard could still hear her.

"What the hell was that?" Maynard asked Jenna.

"I don't know," she said, "but it was close. I can't see you, Maynard. The video feed is shit now. That means the explosion was probably in the communications room with all the hardware and software that links to the array."

"Shit," Maynard spat.

"Oh God, Maynard," Jenna wondered aloud. "Is this thing smart enough to shut off our communications and isolate us?"

There was a secondary explosion. Not as big as the first, but the video link broke and died.

"Jenna!" Maynard yelled and tried to reopen the link, but all he got was static.

CHAPTER 20

Jenna turned to the group of people with her, which numbered nine plus her.

"Okay, folks," she said, "help is coming. They'll be here within ten minutes. We need to reach the airlock and acquire more HEVO suits."

One lady raised her hand and spoke. She appeared shy, but Jenna knew she was a knowledgeable, introverted analyst who could crunch data.

"But we only have two people with suits right now," she said. "And the airlock only has four suits. That means we'll be four suits short if we don't find a few more somewhere else." She posed the dilemma and let it hang in the air.

No one had an answer.

"Does anyone know of any other locations nearby where HEVO suits are stored?" Jenna asked the group. When everyone else exchanged glances of shared ignorance and nobody spoke up, the same lady interjected again.

"I'm sure the maintenance bay has some there. I don't think it's too far away from here either."

"Thank you," Jenna said and pulled out her PDA to access the station map. She said, "Find Maintenance Bay" and the map quickly drew a line from her location to the Maintenance Bay.

"It's practically along the way," Jenna informed them, her voice rising an octave with excitement. "We'll have to hang a right instead of a left at one point and jump a couple of hallways over, but it's not too far out of the way."

"Good," someone said, and all heads nodded in agreement.

Jenna led the way. She followed the map on her PDA, hanging a right, left, and then another right at the intersection where a left would have taken them to the airlock. As they moved through the intersection, off to the left, they heard a loud creaking noise above them. Jenna cringed, a wave of tightening muscles rippling up her spine and neck until it bunched against the base of her skull and lifted her shoulders. She was familiar with this sound now. Far too familiar for her liking. In the last couple of hours, on three different occasions, that same sound had preceded a huge alien tentacle bursting out of an air duct to attack their dwindling group and drag more people to an unspeakable death she wished to God she had never witnessed.

"Run!" Jenna shouted and shoved the introverted girl ahead of her. A moment later, the air duct down the hall blew off the ceiling and implanted in the floor of the hallway. A tentacle ending in a circle made of numerous human hands slammed into the floor and began snaking toward them with terrifying speed, dozens of fingers fanning up and down as it reached for their flesh. Numerous smaller pseudopodia and tentacles erupted from the bulky extremity and extended toward them, stretching, straining to acquire additional biomass to satiate its alien hunger.

The two people already wearing HEVO suits were the slowest … and the first to die.

The smaller tentacles stuck to the two men's heads and snatched them off their feet. The largest tentacle slithered overtop of them. Its cytoplasmic mass enveloped the men, encasing them and bringing them along as it continued to chase the others.

If Jenna had been able to watch, she would have seen the creature snap the suits in half at the waist and twist the helmets off, gaining quicker access to their bodies than it did before on the colony. She would have seen their body parts appear to float through the alien substrate while it rapidly stripped flesh from bone and twisted the larger portions into their smaller component parts before they migrated toward the unseen mass hiding in the station ducts above.

Seconds later, the monster ejected pieces of the mangled HEVO suits from its body, depositing them on the hallway floor in its wake.

Jenna ran for her life, arms pumping as she screamed at the introvert lady in front of her to "Run! Run faster!" Then she shouted, "Turn left!" Jenna made the turn, and slowed just long enough to look back. The two men in the HEVO suits were gone, nowhere in sight. Now she saw several smaller tentacles snatch hold of two ladies and rip them through the air.

One smashed face first into the swollen tentacle mass, its gelatinous tissue smothering her screams before she could breathe in to give them birth. The second woman twisted in mid-air, landed on her back, and sank into the creature's pliable surface structure. The alien organism embraced her body with a burning warmth and pulled her further inward, its surface area expanding to subsume her cellular anatomy within its own. She shrieked in agony and terror as her flesh began to dissolve and bones were wrenched from joints.

Jenna nearly lost control of her bladder. When another man and woman passed by her, she darted down the hallway behind them, sprinting with all her might for the Maintenance Bay entrance. She could hear the creature's flesh sliding across the floor behind her, heard its mass slam into the wall as it turned at the corner to follow them. There was a scream as another lady was snatched in mid-stride.

Jenna looked out ahead. She was maybe twenty meters from the door. The introvert was already inside and waiting to hit the button that would close it once they were through. A gagging sound turned into a muffled cry as the last person in line was caught by the creature.

Now, Jenna was the last in line ... and running for her life.

She saw the other lady and the only man still alive in their group make it inside the bay. Jenna pumped her arms and sprinted with every ounce of energy she possessed. Hands waved her in, and all three of them were yelling for her to "Hurry! Hurry!"

Their eyes were unsure. It was a gamble.

Maybe life was in the cards for Jenna. Maybe death. No guarantees either way. The uncertainty threatened to divide her focus and diminish her efforts in this final sprint for survival. So, Jenna made sure she was pointed in the right direction, then tilted her head back and closed her eyes. She did not want to see her coworker's faces if, suddenly, they changed to reflect that a particularly nasty fate was in store for her.

Jenna ran blindly. Ran like she had never run before, heart thudding in her chest like a sledgehammer as she managed to eke out more speed than her body had ever been willing to grant before.

And then she ran into a man.

He was standing in Jenna's path, positioned to catch her as the bay door shut. A foolish but gentlemanly gesture. Two strides into the Maintenance Bay, Jenna plowed into the man, knocking him flat on the floor before she fell on top of him. As she landed on the man, Jenna heard and felt the violent collision of the monstrous tentacle slamming into the Maintenance Bay double doors mere feet behind her.

There was a resounding *BOOM* as the tentacle assaulted the doors again.

"We need to find a blowtorch," the man underneath her cried out. "We need to weld the doors together before it breaks through."

BOOM.

They scrambled to their feet, and all four of them scurried off in different directions, searching for the proper tool.

BOOM.

"We need a piece of metal too," the man said, "to lay along the seam and weld to the doors."

The introvert saw the hand-held torch first, pointed, and the man rushed to it. He scooped up the tool and ran to the door.

BOOM.

Jenna and the other woman grabbed multiple short metal rods and carried them to the man.

BOOM. The door bulged an inch inward.

The man placed the first metal rod in the middle of the seam where the two doors met, right where it was now bulged slightly apart. He began melting the rod with the torch. It was rushed, sloppy work.

"Do you know how to do this?" Jenna asked the man.

"Not really," he admitted, "but I've watched others do it a hundred times."

He glanced at her, shrugged, and looked back to the work.

"Something's better than nothing, right now, don't cha think?" he asked.

BOOM.

They both startled at the impact, but the bulge did not worsen. Jenna handed him another metal rod, and he continued welding to the top of the door.

"Hey," he called over his shoulder.

"Yeah," Jenna answered. "What do you need?"

"There's two air ducts that feed into this room. Try to find some metal plates big enough to cover them while I finish up here. Oh, and two ladders, if possible.

"Okay," Jenna said. "We're on it."

All three ladies split up in search of the items. By the time the man was done with the door, they had located what he needed and had the ladders in place. Jenna stood atop one ladder, positioned side by side with the other, metal plate in hand. The man climbed up the ladder positioned closest under the air duct. The two of them held the plate in place over the opening and he began welding it to metal ceiling framework.

They finished the first one and hurried to set up for the second one. Jenna was helping him hold the plate against the ceiling, and he was over halfway done when the creaking sound returned above them.

"God no," the man mumbled. "Just one more minute," he pleaded to what he had always believed was an uncaring cosmos.

It didn't change its colors now.

The tentacle slammed into the metal plate, bending it and creating a crack. Human phalanges, joints separated and suspended in the alien cytoplasm, slipped through and curled over the edge of the plate, probing, searching for flesh, for more biomass.

Jenna recoiled on pure instinct.

"Fuck," the man yelped but kept welding. The dense, viscous tissue on top of the fingers began to stretch, small tendrils hunting on feel alone. "Fuck," he said again. "Find me another metal rod. I'm going to need it to fill in this crack."

The introvert rushed off to where she had found the other metal plates earlier.

A howl of pain took them all by surprise. The man bellowed in agony as one of the tendrils found his forearm. He tried to pull away, but it was no use. The other tendrils, informed by the first, seemed to reorient and move in his direction. He reached up and took the hand torch with his left hand and waved it through the air at the approaching tendrils. They shrunk away, but the one attached to his arm remained and was already digesting the upper layers of dermis.

Without any deliberation, the man applied the torch to the tendril on his forearm and held it there. The alien tissue crackled and smoked, then melted as the torch ate a hole through it to reach his own body. He screamed in pain while simultaneously proclaiming his refusal to accept defeat, both to his opponent and himself. A different sizzling sound erupted from the hole in the alien flesh as the pain in his arm increased exponentially. His scream kicked up a few octaves, and he stared at the alien organism, his eyes brimming with tears and desperation, begging it to yield. The smell of his own flesh burning filled his nostrils. The skin blistered and bubbled, then turned black as the torch scorched a path down to the bone, but when the alien creature finally let him go and retreated with the other tendrils back up into the duct, he screamed in triumph.

The man held the torch up to the crack and let the flame reach through into the duct, moving it back and forth to ensure it didn't return to seek him out again.

"Did y'all find more metal rods?" he asked, trying to control his breathing.

"Yes!" The introvert girl shouted as she handed Jenna the metal rod.

"I've got it," Jenna told him.

He pulled the torch back, and she placed the rod over the crack, holding one end while he began welding the other. Despite the agony in his arm, within another minute, he managed to finish welding the plate and rod in place and secured the duct.

The man turned off the torch, handed it to Jenna, and climbed down the ladder. He walked over to a chair at a workbench, sat, and cradled his arm as he cursed and moaned and groaned and thumped his forehead on the counter in between kicking the bench. Anything to help distract himself from the excruciating pain, the literal burning in his arm.

Jenna turned to the two ladies.

"What are your names? I'm Jenna, the chief doctor on the station."

The introvert said, "Laurie," while the other lady said, "Angie."

"Okay, Laurie," Jenna said, "I need you to go locate the HEVO suits and make sure there are at least four of them that are intact and operational. Okay?"

Laurie nodded and hurried off to complete her task.

"Angie, I need your help treating him," Jenna told her. "You good with that?"

"Sure," Angie answered.

Jenna located the med kit, and she and Angie walked over to the man.

"What's your name, sailor?" she asked him. "We'd like to know what to call you since you definitely just saved our asses."

He smiled through a grimace that might as well have been stapled to his face.

"Andy," he said. "And I'm no hero. You got us this far, doc. I just did my part when it was time."

"Oh my," Angie said, "a man with modesty aboard this vessel. I might swoon."

They all chuckled as Jenna located burn gel and a proper bandage.

"This is temporary," Jenna told Andy as she finished applying the dressing and securing it with gauze and tape. "Just enough so we can get you into a HEVO suit before we run out of air in here. Got it? Later, when we get down to the base, I'll fix it up good. Deal?"

Andy looked up at her. "Deal," he agreed.

"I found the suits," Laurie called out. "Over here." Angie and Jenna helped Andy stand, and they walked over to the room where Laurie was waiting.

"Five of them," Laurie said. "All functional."

"All righty then," Jenna said. "Let's get in them. With the air ducts sealed, we'll be running out of air in here soon."

CHAPTER 21

Maynard called Wile-E on the comms when he lost the link with Jenna, his voice strained with fear and impatience.

"How long before we're in position for the spacewalk?" Maynard asked.

"About five minutes," Wile-E assured him.

For Maynard, those next five minutes crawled. It was like he was moving through amber as it hardened. The moments stretched out, seemed to dangle and hang themselves. When he sensed the ship pivot on its nose and swing around to place the bay door in line with the airlock, Maynard finally felt like time had resumed its normal flow.

"In position," Maynard heard Wile-E say over their comms. "Move."

He watched as Bryant and Hurley unbuckled. Cueing off them, Maynard did the same. The three of them transitioned into the bay and proceeded to the door.

"Hook in here, Maynard," Bryant instructed him, indicating a heavy-duty built-in D-ring on the bay wall. "Don't want you getting sucked into the void when we open the door." He turned to smile at Maynard and make sure he got it right. Seeing Maynard was secure, he hooked himself to an anchor point as well. Hurley was already attached. Maynard knew they would depressurize the bay before the door opened. There would be no sudden vacuum pulling at their bodies when the door opened. Bryant just wanted to fuck with him a little to break the tension he was feeling.

"We're secure," Bryant announced to Wile-E. "Depressurizing now." Bryant grabbed the handle and levered it downward, initiating depressurization. When complete, a large button on the wall nearby flashed green and released the safety mechanism. Bryant hammered the green button with his gloved fist, and the bay door began to rise.

Maynard activated the video link and tried to contact Jenna again.

"Jenna? Are you there?" he asked and waited for her response while Bryant stepped forward first, grabbed the tether cable, attached it to his suit, and jumped out of the ship. He didn't fall, he simply floated toward the station. Hurley stepped forward and hooked himself to the tether cable and leapt out of the ship, following perhaps three meters behind Bryant.

"Jenna?" Maynard repeated. "We're here. Bryant and Hurley are making the spacewalk now. You copy?"

Bryant activated the jet pack thrusters built into the HEVO suit, and Hurley did the same. Maynard could see the thrusters firing for one to two seconds, then cutting out for a few seconds before Bryant fired them again. The man was adjusting the direction of the thrusters by minute increments as he drew closer to the station. Bryant steered himself in, on course for a perfect landing, while Hurley trailed behind him, waiting for Bryant to land and secure the tether cable.

A weak, vibratory force struck Bryant, then Hurley a second later, and Maynard a couple of seconds after that. Nothing severe. Kind of like a ripple in a pond.

"What the fuck was that?" Bryant asked.

"No idea," replied Hurley.

Maynard analyzed the sensation of force which had struck him, considered it and compared it to known things he had experienced in his life during mining operations where they used explosives or gigantic jackhammer devices. It took him several seconds, and Bryant was only two meters from landing when it hit him.

That was an impact force ripple, he thought to himself. Oh shit …

"Bryant, Hurley!" Maynard shouted into the comms. "That was an impact force ripple."

"What do you mean?" Bryant asked.

"You know," Maynard explained, "like a hammer hitting metal hard and you feel it when you're right next to it. That alien thing must have hit something inside the station ... *hard* ... and nearby."

"Fuck," said Bryant, as he landed on the station platform and activated his magnetic boots. Bryant pulled the anchor plate and bolt driver from off his thigh. He placed the plate against the platform, lined up the tool with the hole, and squeezed the trigger. A thick bolt drove into the station. He repeated the process in each of the other three holes. A metal ring hung from the plate. Bryant removed the tether cable hook from his suit and attached it to the ring on the anchor plate.

"Line is set and secure," he announced to the others. "You got your lady on the video link yet, Maynard?" Bryant asked him.

"I'm trying!" Maynard responded.

Bryant and Hurley felt the vibratory force again, except this time it rattled their bodies where they now both stood on the platform. They looked at each other.

"That ain't good," Bryant stated with a dry bluntness. Hurley shook his head in negative agreement.

"Jenna!" Maynard yelled into his headset. "Jenna! For God's sake, are you there? Come in! Come in! We're ready to receive you at the airlock door. Do you copy?"

Snow and static appeared in the upper corner of his HUD as the video link tried to open but was only partially successful. Scratchy squawks and screeches pierced Maynard's ears. The pattern of sounds resembled that of someone speaking, but it was entirely unintelligible.

"Jenna!" he said, "if you can copy me, we're coming inside to get you. Get as close to the airlock as possible. We're coming for you."

Maynard grabbed his Pumpkin Puncher shotgun, unhooked from the ship, and attached himself to the tether cable stretching across space to the station. He stepped out into the blackness of space and activated the jets on his suit. Steering was unnecessary. The line would guide him in.

"I can't make out her transmission, guys," Maynard said. "We gotta go inside and get her. Comms should be better in there if she's not too far away. These things can transmit audio direct within the station without using the communications array."

Bryant and Hurley turned toward the ship to see Maynard en route to their location. They watched and waited as he completed his spacewalk. Once Maynard touched down, he activated his gravity boots and unhooked from the tether cable.

"What do you think you're doing?" Bryant asked Maynard.

"I'm going in with you guys to get her," Maynard informed the man.

"That was not part of the plan," Bryant replied. "You're supposed to stay out here."

"Well, I can't reach her, so the plan has changed. I'm coming inside." Maynard stated his intentions with an unflinching conviction.

Bryant eyed Maynard with a side-long glance.

"For fuck sake, dude," Bryant said, "just don't shoot us in the back, ya hear?"

"Not on accident, I won't," Maynard said and chuckled. He hefted the shotgun and held it in a low ready position—butt of the stock welded to his shoulder, the barrel pointing toward the ground, his thumb resting on the safety, and index finger off the trigger. Just like Cody had instructed him. "All right. Let's go," he said.

Hurley approached the data entry panel and keyed in a code he had pulled from the specs he accessed through the station's memory cloud.

ACCESS DENIED flashed across the screen.

"What the hell?" Hurley muttered and tried it again, making sure he didn't make a mistake.

ACCESS DENIED.

"Well shit," he said. "We're locked out. Code doesn't work."

"What do you mean it doesn't work?" Maynard asked without thinking, agitation, fear, and impatience getting the best of him.

"It ain't rocket science, dude," Hurley said. "It's not accepting our code. Access has been restricted somehow. But no problem. I came prepared for just such a situation."

Hurley keyed in a code on his forearm, and a small opening popped up on the upper left arm of his HEVO suit. He retrieved an item from inside and stepped over to where he knew the door locking mechanism sat behind the wall. He pressed something and twisted the item, then placed it on the wall. A built-in magnet kept it in place.

"What's that?" Maynard asked.

"Shaped charge," Hurley said, reaching over his shoulder to pull a three-foot-long rod-like object off his back. He gripped the handle on one end and thumbed a button forward. A metal sail unfurled, rotating counterclockwise like a large fan opening until it had come full circle and intersected with the rod. The metal material tightened as the circuit closed, its structure becoming firmer just as its purpose became clear to Maynard. A shield.

"Stack up behind me, boys," Hurley said, and both Bryant and Maynard did so without question.

"Heads down in case of shrapnel," Hurley instructed, and a moment later, calm as could be, "Fire in the hole. Three ... two ... one ..."

BOOM!

Most of the force was directed into the station, but enough residual shock rebounded off the wall to cause Maynard's teeth to chatter for a second or two.

"Pull her open, Bryant," Hurley said.

Bryant stepped forward, activated magnets in his gloves, and gripped the door in the middle to one side of the crack where the two halves met. He heaved, and both doors moved along their tracks freely now that the locking mechanism no longer held them captive.

"Shield first," Hurley said. "Fall in behind me."

Hurley drew the flame unit one-handed, prepped it, and pointed it ahead of them, resting it on a notch jutting out of the right side of the shield. It was designed to allow a shield bearer to carry a larger weapon and not just a sidearm.

Maynard fell in on Hurley's heels, and Bryant brought up the rear.

"We're up," said Bryant after seeing Maynard was ready.

"Going in," Hurley announced as he walked forward, his steps slow and steady. "Eyes sharp, boys." Once they moved inside, Hurley spoke again. "Maynard, try to raise your girl on the video comm link now that we've entered the station."

"Will do," Maynard answered, looking around. Everything appeared normal in this area. No damage. They moved through the hallway slowly, scanning for any sign of people or the alien creature.

"Jenna," Maynard called out. "Jenna, can you hear me?" A moment later, his headset crackled, and a female voice spoke. It was somewhat broken by periodic static, but he could make out Jenna's words for the most part.

"Yes!" she cried, almost hissing into the mic, trying to keep her voice down but speak loud enough for Maynard to make her words out. "I'm here, Maynard. I'm here."

Maynard's heart leapt with hope, and a boulder of dread rolled off his chest at the sound of Jenna speaking.

"I can hear you, babe," Maynard said, his voice excited and relieved all at once.

Hurley and Bryant stopped and waited for intel. No need to plow forward past turn offs and have to backtrack.

"Where are you at?" Maynard asked. "What happened? We just entered the station at the communication's array airlock, as planned. Tell me where you are so we can come get you."

"Maynard," Jenna said, "we're hiding in the Maintenance Bay. Right after we ended communications earlier, the damn thing dropped a huge tentacle out of an air duct into our hallway, blocking our evac route. We had to divert here and take shelter. We quick welded the door shut so it can't be opened by any entered code, then welded metal plating over the air ducts to hopefully block all access. It cut us off from life support, but thankfully there were five HEVO suits in here. We went ahead and put them on."

"How many are with you?" Maynard asked. "And where exactly is this maintenance bay located in relation to the airlock?"

"Me plus three," Jenna said. "Out of all the people I could collect along the way, only three survived. There may be some others left alive, hiding God knows where on the station, but I have no idea where they might be, and I don't think there's any way you could reach them without dying in the process. That thing has branched out everywhere. It was in the hallway outside the Maintenance Bay about five minutes ago, pounding away on the door and walls. They buckled and caved in some but held long enough for it to give up, but I'm sure it's looking for another way in. I suspect it will be pounding on the metal plates we welded over the air ducts any time now."

"Okay," affirmed Maynard. "Got it. Now, where exactly are you located? What's the quickest route to you?"

"From the airlock," Jenna explained, "think of it like a capital *E*. You're at the tip of the top line of the *E*. Head down the hallway, take the first left you get to, then take the second left after that, and go until you see a large double door. That's the Maintenance Bay. But Maynard, I'm serious …" Concern filled Jenna's voice, and Maynard could sense the fear creeping in as well. "That *thing* is out there … and it's hungry as hell. Be careful. Don't die on me."

Maynard swallowed hard. It was time to cowboy up and make a difference. He might die a horrible death, but he knew that already. When he decided to push the bill and come up here on a rescue mission, he knew there was a strong possibility he might die trying to do right. A cold chill struck him. He shivered briefly and shook it off.

"I won't die on you, Jenna," he assured her. "We're coming. Be ready to cut that door open and run."

CHAPTER 22

They made their way down the hallway in a slight zig zag formation. Hurley took the lead and positioned himself in the center of the hall with the shield. Maynard was in the middle and offset to his right, while Bryant brought up rear security, offset to the left. This provided a flame unit in the lead and one covering their asses. Each of them turned up their audio boosters so their outside mics would amplify any sound the creature might make in the duct work and forewarn them as soon as possible.

Hurly paused, gradually clearing the corner at the first left.

Nothing.

They made the turn and proceeded at a cautious pace, minimizing the noise generated by their footfalls and listening intently for any sign of the alien beast lurking unseen nearby. Maynard's heart pounded in his chest, in his ears. His breathing was threatening to run amok on him. His body wanted to run. To sprint to Jenna's location and run like hell for the exit once he had her. Slow movement was so much worse. It seemed like inaction, like molasses dripping over the bark of a tree. Maynard felt like a snail fleeing through a field of trap door spiders, any of which might leap out and drag him to his death at any given moment.

Sweat trickled down the crack of Maynard's ass and forced a shivering chill up his spine. Larger beads of sweat ran along the side of his face while the skullcap covering his forehead became soaked.

"For fuck's sake," Maynard muttered. "Can we move any slower? We're sitting ducks."

"Stay calm, man," Bryant encouraged him, nearly reading Maynard's mind. "Steady and quiet. Maintain your composure. Running is what predators want their prey to do. It reveals their location and tells the hunter their fear has overcome their intellect. Their ability to control themselves has collapsed. So, if you choose to run when the predator is nearby, you'll be easier pickings unless you're faster than the average gazelle."

Bryant waited a moment and spoke again to Maynard.

"Control your breathing," he instructed the miner who had no combat experience. "Breathe in for one, two, three, four. Hold one, two, three, four. Breathe out one, two, three, four. Again. In one, two, three, four. Hold one, two, three, four. Out one, two, three, four."

Bryant continued whispering the count for Maynard to follow as they took each step, rolling their boots slowly from heel to toe then lifting it from heel to toe. The movement of his left foot synced with the breathing count. Stepping down, heel, one, two, three, four. Toes touching and heel lifting, one, two, three, four. Toes leaving the floor and foot moving through the air, one, two, three, four, until the foot touched down again and heel, one, two, three, four began again.

Maynard counted this off for five cycles until Hurley cleared the first intersection and they began moving again. Maynard's left foot was half-way to toes touching down when Hurley stopped suddenly. Maynard heard the noise too. They all did. A loud creak above them and maybe five meters down the hallway to their left.

They froze. Every muscle tightened to lock itself in place. Maynard's neck craned beneath the weight of terror looming above him, as if he were a field mouse when it has seen the shadow of the hawk fly overhead and the poor creature attempts to look up while hugging the ground, immobile, its beady black eyes searching the sky to locate the threat.

Maynard tried to look up as well, canting his head to the left, eyes cutting to the far edge of his vision so hard they shook. His neck and head trembled as well while they waited, the seconds ticking away. He was desperate to put his finger on the trigger of his shotgun and point it … somewhere … anywhere. He wanted to start shooting into the air ducts above. Take action. Go on the offensive. Not sit here and wait to be attacked.

The waiting. For God's sake, the waiting was too much. Too much. His whole body quivered in disobedience to the adrenaline pumping into his system, commanding him to fight or flee. Hurley and Bryant experienced the same angst but knew the symptoms, had experience with fighting the urges.

"Hurley," Bryant whispered. "He's about to lose it."

Maynard was oblivious to their exchange, but he noticed Bryant's hand pull gently on the D ring mounted to the back of his HEVO suit in between his shoulder blades and he saw Hurley stretch the flame unit out to his right side as if to block any forward movement.

"Hold," Hurley said, and nothing else.

Maynard held. They listened. There was another creak further down the hallway. They waited for another eternity, it seemed to Maynard, and when no other sound came, Hurley placed the flame unit barrel back on its perch and advanced forward.

Stepping forward, Maynard's legs were wobbly and weak. It took a concerted effort to prevent them from buckling and causing him to stumble forward. He stalled for a moment, then started up again and had to stutter step to keep from falling forward uncontrolled. He planted the balls of his feet twice and then a third time before catching himself.

"Goddammit!" Hurley hissed. "Heel to toe, Maynard. Heel to toe," he whispered.

Maynard thought they would stop and listen again, but Hurley kept putting one foot in front of the other.

"Oh, fuck me," Maynard said. "That's two HEVO suits on the floor up ahead, isn't it?"

"Yes," Hurley responded, "and there's two sets of clothes a little further up. Ignore it, Maynard. Focus on the job."

Maynard gulped and tried not to stare at the jagged edges of the suits where they were torn apart as he walked by them.

Ten meters later, they reached the next intersection. Hurley slowed long enough to peek around the corner and continued, making the left-hand turn and moving toward the end of the hall, where they could all see the double bay doors Jenna had described to Maynard.

"Another set of clothes here," Hurley informed everyone. "Door is in sight. Maynard, tell your girl we're almost to them."

Maynard activated the video link.

"Jenna? You there?" Maynard asked quietly.

Jenna's face popped up in the corner of his HUD.

"I'm here."

"Good," Maynard replied. "So are we. We're on final approach now and have the door in sight."

"Tell her to begin cutting through the weld on the door they did earlier," Hurley ordered Maynard.

Jenna heard the traffic inside Maynard's helmet and answered.

"Copy that," Jenna responded. "Andy, you're up," she said.

Andy stepped forward with the blowtorch and began tracing a line down the middle, burning through the metal rod he had welded to the door earlier.

"And tell her to sync their comms with ours," Hurley said. "I'm syncing now."

"I copied that as well," Jenna informed Maynard before he had a chance to relay the information. "Everyone hit sync on your comms," she instructed.

"Andy's almost done," Jenna updated Maynard. "Ladies," she ordered, "stack up behind me. Okay. Opening the door in five, four, three, two, one."

Maynard, Hurley, and Bryant watched the double bay doors spread apart and all three of them cringed inside their suits at the volume of noise generated by the hydraulic pistons working.

"Oh fuck," Hurley said with exasperated disgust. "No way the creature missed *that* racket."

Hurley waved Jenna and the others to move.

"Hurry up, people. Fill in the middle behind me and follow my lead."

Hurley turned around and, without delay, began moving back the way they had just come. Maynard made eye contact with Jenna and nudged her with one hand, indicating she should go first. There was no way he was risking her getting left behind if they had to run. Angie, Laurie, and Andy fell in behind Maynard while Bryant brought up the rear.

Maynard was happy their pace was slightly faster, but it wasn't fast enough for his liking. The sound of metal creaking and crumpling as the alien mass moved through the ducts toward the bay door reverberated above them. They had to move as fast as they could quietly manage. Too slow and they wouldn't round the corner before the creature popped out of the ducts into the hall. Too fast and they would make enough noise to draw its attention, for sure.

Hurley balanced the odds and kept them moving nice and steady. They rounded the first corner, taking a right onto the long, straight stretch of hallway. Bryant had just made the turn when a loud crash resounded behind him, followed by what sounded like a giant aluminum can crumpling. The alien creature's tentacle billowed in size as it exited the duct, swelling from almost a meter in diameter to over two meters, rupturing the ceiling of the hallway like someone tearing tissue paper apart.

Bryant didn't stop to look back.

"Bogie just entered the hallway by the bay doors," Bryant advised. "And fuck it sounds big."

"Copy that," Hurley responded. "Maintain pace, and hopefully, it won't hear us yet. Let me know if it starts closing on us."

"Roger that," Bryant answered. "Will do."

Maynard had made out the noise of the alien creature landing in the hallway all too clearly with his exterior mic turned up. The sound rattled his eardrums, and though he'd never believed in God, the phrase "put the fear of God in them" now held new meaning for him. He didn't think this monster was a god, but it certainly could appear that way when compared to their fragile flesh and feeble bones. Their vulnerability before this beast was absolute. To them, it was a god of hunger and wrath, of bludgeoning violence which could not be placated or stopped.

The hallway had become a blur amidst Maynard's racing thoughts. It was a blessing. They were past the first intersection and nearing the next one ahead where they would turn right and move to the exit.

Fucking hell, Maynard thought. I'm not ready to die. And I definitely don't want to die like this. I'd rather suffocate in space.

"Bryant!" Maynard blurted out, unable to be quiet any longer. "What can you hear back there?"

"It just moved back into the air ducts. I heard the metal shearing as it retracted its mass back inside."

"It's coming?" Maynard asked, terror filling his voice.

"I don't know," Bryant said, "but it knows we're not in the bay, and it might know where the exit—"

There was a sudden explosion of noise from the hallway branching off the intersection behind them. It was the shrieking sound of metal rending, ripping open, and blowing into pieces that perforated the walls and punched a huge hole into the floor. The force was similar to a gigantic cannonball accelerating at a dizzying rate to blast through the ceiling, then decelerating before it could penetrate through the floor to the next level.

"Oh fuck," Bryant said, then he and Maynard together, "It's coming! Run!"

The time for stealth was over. Primal instincts sprang into action at last, every heart pumping wildly as fear-filled impulses drove their bodies into action. Boots thudded in a cacophony of pounding noises as each man and woman ran at their own fastest pace.

Except Bryant, who remained in the rear and moved as fast as the slowest person would allow him, voluntarily becoming the guy most likely to be eaten by the pursuing bear in a wilderness survival scenario.

Maynard moved with clarity of thought and action, this being the second time today he had run for his life in the bulky HEVO suit. He kept Jenna in front of him and didn't care about anyone else. She was the reason he was here. She was his reason for risking life and limb and a horrifically painful death. He focused on her and kept moving.

They felt as much as heard the walls and floor warp and twist around them. The alien tentacle filled the hallway, then swelled larger still, pushing itself forward in pursuit of its prey, stretching every structure around it as if it were rubber instead of metal.

Maynard careened around the corner, his feet sliding as his weight pushed him outward, until he struck the wall and bounced off. He staggered, stumbled, reached out with his left hand to steady himself on the wall, all while never stopping forward movement. Angie and Andy passed him up by the time he was moving out at top speed again, while Laurie was only a meter or so behind him now. The exit was up ahead. Maybe fifty meters. That was it.

We're close! Maynard told himself. *Don't stop.*

Seconds later, the massive alien tentacle slammed into the wall, just like Maynard had done but with a devastating impact, crushing the metal even as its morphing form pulled itself along, gripping at every surface for leverage to continue chasing after them.

"Laying down fire!" Maynard heard Bryant shout, and he actually stopped to turn and look. Laurie mimicked his behavior without thinking.

A wall of flame filled the hallway, tentacles of every size flailing within the fire as it burned them. Something inhuman screeched in pain as Bryant backed away, finger never lifting from the trigger as he waved the weapon's barrel side to side, roiling flames licking the alien flesh, charring it blacker with every second. The creature had slowed to a crawl, but it wasn't stopping.

It wasn't stopping at all.

You dumbass, Maynard screamed inside his head. It's not stopping. You can't stop. Run!

"Run!" Maynard yelled out loud and turned to do so, his eyes briefly seeing the shock-filled face of Laurie as his visor panned past her.

"Run, Bryant!" Maynard yelled this time as he looked forward and realized everyone had stopped to look back when he did. They were *not* several meters further closer to the exit like they *should* have been.

"Run, Jenna!" Maynard barked. "Run and don't stop! Don't stop!" His voice commanded and, at the same time, pleaded with her.

And then they saw the vent cover closest to the airlock blow off the ceiling.

A fraction of a second later, alien flesh filled the corridor. The bulging end of a huge tentacle unfurled like a sunflower, revealing twelve heads. They all screamed, tongues trumpeting in rage and ravenous hunger. Twenty-four pupils swelled and contracted in the milky white orbs that held them, their gaze malevolent and full of only one purpose.

Consumption.

"Stop, Jenna! Stop!" Maynard stepped in front of her even as Hurley knelt on one knee, planting the shield on the floor and squeezing the trigger to unleash hell.

Maynard witnessed the indifference to human life in those once human eyes before the alien heads curled inward to protect themselves from the fiery blaze. *We're just food,* he thought, *and this thing is hungry as fuck. The evolutionary food chain has just been reordered, folks.*

But Maynard wasn't ready to give up yet. He shouldered the shotgun with the white phosphorus rounds and yelled "Fuck you too!"

Maynard pulled the trigger as fast as his finger could move, pumping the burning rounds into the creature's tentacle head and then the flesh beneath it as it reared up in pain. Behind him, Bryant pulled out the belt of white phosphorus grenades, and hollered, "Fire in the hole!" He ripped a cord out and threw them all at the alien mass creeping toward him. They embedded in its flesh and were immediately absorbed inside. Bryant threw up one more wall of flame then turned and ran.

The white phosphorus shells Maynard fired burned inside the tentacle while Hurley's flame unit roasted and charred the outside. Between the two of them, they were driving it back, forcing it to retreat. Hurley stood and advanced, and Maynard followed his example. Muffled alien cries and high-pitched shrieks peeled forth from the creature as it finally withdrew inside the vent. Hurley lifted the shield over his head and poured flames into the opening, preventing it from returning.

"Go!" he shouted at Maynard. "Get everyone outside and attached to the tether cable. Now!"

Maynard pushed Jenna past Hurley and toward the airlock, then turned back and waved the others to follow them. Jenna opened the airlock and they rushed inside and closed it. Maynard instantly pulled the lever to decompress and counted the seconds off as they stared at the exit. When he reached ten, the outer door opened, and they moved outside. Once everyone was clear, Maynard closed the door so Hurley and Bryant could move inside the airlock. The locking mechanism was blown to hell, but the door would still close and remain shut.

Maynard helped Jenna attach to the guideline and told her to activate the rear thrusters.

He slapped her on the back of her suit.

"Go! I'll be right behind you."

Maynard hitched himself to the line and turned to assist the others. Angie and Andy were there waiting but Laurie wasn't in sight.

"What the hell?" he said out loud. "I thought Laurie was with us."

"What?" exclaimed Jenna. "What do you mean?"

"She's not out here. She must not have made it inside the airlock before we shut the door."

"No," Maynard heard Bryant say. "She's still in here with us. We got her. Don't worry. Just get your asses moving to the ship." Bryant paused then finished, "That's an order."

"You don't have to tell me twice," Maynard said, then grabbed Angie's tether line and hooked it to the cable stretching toward their ship. Andy watched and imitated, successfully hooking himself to the cable as well. Maynard pointed to the rear and forward thruster buttons on the wrist controls.

"Make sure you use the forward thruster to slow down when you get close to the ship. You don't want to go splat."

With that, he turned and hit his rear thruster button and took off toward the dropship behind Jenna.

CHAPTER 23

Hurley was still filling the air duct with flames when Bryant moved past him.

"Last man!" Bryant yelled as he stepped past Hurley and opened the airlock door. "Now, move your ass, Hurley! There's an even bigger fucker coming down the hallway.

"I got it!" Hurley hollered in response, and turned to back into the airlock, making sure a steady stream of hell poured into the hallway to continue slowing the alien organism. Bryant stood beside him and added his weapon's flames to the fire. The creature nearly stopped for a few seconds, its outer layers crisping, turning black, and peeling away, which in turn allowed the next layer to be charred as well.

One layer of dermis at a time, they were cooking the monster, and yet, still, it's will to feed was indomitable. It shrugged the mounting injuries off and continued crawling forward, a mere handful of meters away now.

Hurley closed the door. Bryant pulled the lever to decompress.

One, two, three …

The alien flesh slammed into the airlock door, causing the whole door to crumple inward by a few inches.

"Get them out of here!" Hurley commanded Bryant, pulling rank.

Four, five …

"Fuck that, boss!" Bryant argued. "You have skills they may need. I'm just a grunt. Get your ass out of here!"

Six, seven …

BOOM!

A huge dent, a foot in diameter and half as deep, appeared in the center of the door.

Eight, nine, ten …

The outer door opened at last, and Laurie hurried to exit the airlock. She noticed the others were already crossing the chasm between the station and the dropship.

Hurley looked at Bryant for a moment, anger in his eyes but also the recognition that Bryant was right. His EOD training and knowledge could be crucial in the fight ahead of them. He nodded and handed the shield to Bryant.

"Take this, and don't lollygag in hopes of greater glory. You feel me, Bryant?"

"Who me?" Bryant said as he took the shield, dropped the flame unit, and drew the belt fed shotgun from his back.

Hurley slapped Bryant's back and said, "Last man," then turned and moved to the cable, where he helped get Laurie attached to it first. Once she activated her rear thrusters, Hurley prepared to evac as well. He turned to face the station, hooked onto the cable, and activated his forward thrusters. He holstered the flamer, drew his shotgun, and held it at a low ready position while watching Bryant back out the door now.

"Don't stop moving, Bryant!" Hurley ordered. "Just hook on as you are and hit your forward thrusters."

"I'm on it, boss!" Bryant said. "Ain't no give up in my game!"

BOOM!

The internal airlock door blew off the wall and straight into Bryant, striking the shield and sending him flying backwards off the platform. The force of impact slammed through his body. The memory of a wave pile-driving him at the beach once blossomed inside his brain, but he kept his senses about him and remained focused.

Releasing the shield, Bryant accessed his suit's tether line and brought the hook down on the cable with only an inch to spare, then activated his forward thrusters. He raised the shotgun and thumbed the selector to full auto right as the alien creature erupted from the station, a huge tentacle bursting out of the airlock as others simultaneously forced their way through the hull beneath the comms array, and a huge amorphous shape emerged from the fissures close behind them.

Bryant aimed at the tentacle following him out of the airlock and fired, holding down the trigger as he did so. A barrage of white phosphorus assaulted the alien creature, tearing into its flesh to burn deep within. The tentacles bifurcated again and again, splitting and dividing to twist and wind as they attempted to evade the agonizing white phosphorous and reach Bryant.

So it could feed.

"Fuck you, motherfucker!" Bryant yelled while straining to control the recoil as he continued to fire without ceasing.

But even as he did so, the tentacles split into smaller and smaller pieces and managed to evade his attack more efficiently ... began to gain on him, and fast.

"Oh fuck," he said.

The multitude of tentacles suddenly rushed forward, closing the distance with rapidity.

"Maynard!" Bryant called out as death fell upon him, hundreds of tiny tentacles wrapping and intertwining all about his suit, tightening about the neck where helmet and torso connected. "By the bay door! Grab the big RPG and shoot this fucker! Now!"

A loud crack, followed by wet gurgling noises and slithering sounds, filled Maynard and Hurley's ears.

"Goddamn bastard!" Hurley said and choked up at the sight of his partner's grotesque death, the tentacles filling the man's suit and dissecting it all at once, flaying the human flesh into slices the alien flesh quickly absorbed.

Maynard was glad he hadn't seen Bryant die, but he heard the man's last words and was anxious to obey.

Jenna was climbing into the ship's cargo bay and Maynard was only about ten seconds from reaching the entrance. He called out to her.

"Did you copy Bryant's last traffic to me, Jenna?" he asked.

"Yes," she said. "Where is it at?"

"I don't know. I think he said it's in a storage compartment by the bay door.

"Which side?"

"The other side of the bay from where you're at now, Jenna" Hurley said. "Red handle. Twist then pull out and down to open the compartment. It's *big*. You can't miss it."

"Gotcha," Jenna said, then unhooked and made her way across the bay.

The alien thing continued to expand its form outside the station while the body remained anchored inside. Three columns of flesh sprouted up. Each one ended in the sunflower shape with twelve heads unfurling to announce their growing fury. The many tentacles stretching toward Hurley and the ship beyond contorted and came back together, coiling into one huge tentacle, which then divided into two massive tentacle arms. They rushed to reach for them as the thirty-six heads bellowed a single command.

"Caahnn uuuunto neeeeee!" the creature cried into the void of space, but Hurley had no way to know that it spoke. It repeated the cry, the words churning with rage at Hurley's defiance of their demand. The tentacle arms lunged forward and, continuing to grow at an alarming rate, sped toward Hurley. He pulled the trigger rapid fire, filling the space between them with white phosphorus. The creature's limbs recoiled momentarily as their flesh ripped and sizzled, then pushed ahead, absorbing the burning phosphorus, indifferent to the pain.

Maynard set foot on the bay floor, unhooked himself from the cable, and moved to accept the RPG from Jenna, who was now holding it, arms outstretched toward him.

"God, this sucker is *huge*, Maynard!" Jenna exclaimed, proffering the weapon to him.

It dwarfed her petite frame and was far longer than she was tall. The rocket shaped grenade inserted into the launcher was bigger around than a basketball at the center point, then tapered on each end, stretching nearly one meter in overall length. It looked more like a warhead than a grenade. Including the launcher, the weapon was easily two and a half meters long.

"Holy shit," Maynard said, then took it, turned, and knelt.

"I've got the RPG!" Maynard announced.

Flipping up the targeting reticule, he aimed it toward the station and the center of the three stalks upon which sat the alien's heads.

"Wait for it to lock on, Maynard," Hurley said, still holding down the trigger to fend off the approaching alien arms, which were drawing far too near for Hurley's comfort.

"Anytime you're ready to fire is good with me," Hurley said, watching both tentacle arms hurry toward him.

The reticle flashed red and chirped inside Maynard's helmet twice, then informed him, "Target Lock Acquired."

"This is for Bryant, you fucker," Maynard said and fired the RPG.

The warhead launched, rocketing through space at an increasing speed. Hurley watched it zoom past him even as the alien arms drew closer.

Hurley stared after the rocket propelled grenade, then closed his eyes. He hoped it would strike the creature before the thing had a chance to kill him, but he did not want to see his potential death coming either.

Pain flared like a supernova in Hurley's ankle as something crushed the joint with ease. The sickening pain took his breath. He felt a tug, and his body started to reverse course.

A second later, the shockwave from the RPG exploding struck Hurley, jolting his body within the suit, but the force did not move him through space, did not counteract the effort pulling him back toward the station.

Not one bit.

In fact, the pressure encircling his ankle tightened, clamping down just above the joint.

CHAPTER 24

Maynard watched the RPG pass Hurley and home in on the alien. It struck the central stalk a couple of meters beneath the head and blew. The blast force decapitated the center head and radiated outward, destroying everything nearby that Maynard had not seen as he focused in on shooting the monster.

The main satellite dish and antennae of the communication's array were shredded and torn from the hull. The twisted pieces tumbled away from the station and out of sight.

The creature thrashed and flailed in pain but did not allow the severed head to float away.

The alien flesh gripping Hurley's ankle suddenly spasmed with tremendous force and sheered through the end of his shin, crinkling the suit shut around the stump inside. Both tentacle arms retreated from Hurley, his right foot and boot absorbing into its biomass as they reached back through space for their drifting third head, caught it, and dragged it back down to the station, where they reattached it to the central stalk once more.

Hurley's thrusters moved him toward the ship again. A few large globules of deep, bright red blood floated in space behind him, but that was all. As Hurley drew closer, Maynard could see the severed suit leg was pinched tightly closed where his comrade's missing foot should have been.

"I'm okay," Hurley reassured Maynard when he reached the bay door. "Just need to get out of this and make sure we stop the bleeding. I think where that damned creature twisted it off, the suit is acting like a partial tourniquet."

"Fucking hell," Maynard said, looking at Hurley. "I thought you were a goner for sure."

"Not today, I guess," Hurley said. "Teamwork."

Hurley gave Maynard a fist bump, then turned and hit the button to close the bay door. Once it finished shutting, Maynard told the others to pick a seat and buckle in, then helped Hurley over to a seat and secured him. Maynard sat next to Jenna and buckled himself in.

"We're all secured," Maynard said.

"You hear that, Wile-E?" Hurley asked, breathing heavily.

"That I did," Wile-E answered.

"Good," Hurley said. "Now get us the hell out of here and back to base."

"And let them know we need medical personnel present on our arrival for a loss of limb injury," Maynard added.

Back on board the station, the alien creature roared with human tongues into the void of space and flailed tentacles in a fit of rage at its escaping prey. Their ship's thrusters carried the craft away, leaving it to watch them descend toward the exomoon's surface, powerless to stop them.

The amalgam twitched and undulated, its form morphing and rearranging itself in seemingly random ways until it could detect the humans no more. Afterward, it retreated inside the station through the airlock and the multiple holes ripped in the hull when it emerged. As its immense mass maneuvered away from the hull and allowed the vacuum of space access to the station, sensors detected a loss of atmosphere. Bulkhead doors slammed shut, sealing the rest of the station off to preserve oxygen and maintain life support, though there were no other human beings on board now.

The creature made its way slowly to the bridge, accessing information from Commander Cranston's brain, determined to use any knowledge it could obtain to develop a thorough understanding of the technological systems used by these creatures.

In time, it might deduce a way off the station.

CHAPTER 25

As they descended toward the surface, Maynard leaned back in his seat, eyes closed, his right hand gripping Jenna's left.

"Fucking hell," he said aloud and muted himself to everyone but Jenna. "That ... thing. That thing killed a lot of good people today."

He felt Jenna's hand squeeze his own.

"I'm so sorry it ended up on the station with you, baby" Maynard confessed. "I'm so sorry ... but ... it was the best chance for the most colonists to survive. Cody was right ... and he died for it. But I'm so thankful for the Recovery Team. Bryant died rescuing you. He's a fucking hero. More than I could ever be."

"What are you talking about?" Jenna asked him. "You saved us with that RPG shot ... or at the very least, you saved Hurley. Don't sell yourself short."

Maynard shook his head.

"But I wasn't brave, not like Bryant. That guy looked death in the face and didn't flinch. I was scared as fuck the whole damn time, from the second we stepped foot inside that station until the very end ... I was scared as fuck. I almost lost it. I think I would have at one point if it weren't for Bryant. That guy was a fucking bad-ass warrior. A hero. No doubt."

"No argument there," Jenna said. "But fear doesn't make you any less brave. If you do the deeds ... and you did ... it doesn't matter if you did it afraid. You're still brave in my book. You're still a hero to me."

She squeezed his hand once more, and he squeezed hers back tightly, then they sat in silence the rest of the way back to base.

Back on base, medical attended to Hurley's amputated foot, while Wile-E, Maynard, and Jenna made their way to Dispatch. As they walked through the door, Wile-E spoke.

"Have you received any communications from HQ since the last thing you advised of before launch?"

Bill Reid shook his head.

"No, sir. Nothing."

"Run a long-range comms check," Wile-E instructed. "I'm pretty sure we're fucked, but let's verify it to make it official."

Bill looked at him, confused.

"We destroyed the communications array on the station in the process of escaping," Wile-E said bluntly.

Bill's mouth formed a big O, then closed.

"Aye aye, sir. Will do."

As they stood there waiting, Maynard experienced a twinge of guilt but knew it couldn't have been helped. There had been no other choice.

"I'm afraid you're right, sir," Bill announced a minute later. "Long-range comms are definitely down. What now?"

"What now?" Wile-E asked in response. "Now we hurry up and wait ... and act like everything is normal until the Queen Antares arrives to rescue our asses from this rock."

"What about the other two eggs, Wile-E?" Maynard asked. "What should we do with them?"

"Leave 'em the fuck where they are," Wile-E said. "They laid in that ship harmless for God knows how long before Rich Maloy decided to cut into one of them. They can lay right there untouched as far as I'm concerned. No one goes near that ship. If they do, I'll shoot them myself on sight. Spread the word."

"Copy that, sir," Maynard said. "Sounds like the voice of reason to me. A rare sound around here too."

"So, what does that mean for everyone?" Jenna asked.

"Well, for most everyone here," Maynard began to explain, "it means business as usual. HQ sent a communication earlier telling us that the normal mining operations should be maintained while we await extraction."

"Okay," Jenna followed up. "And what does that mean for us?"

"Well, for me," Maynard said, and gave her a sly smile, "it means my job is done and I'm officially on a six-month vacation. You, on the other hand, should be able to take some time off with me and help out the doc down here as needed. I say we kick off our vacation with a shower, then a long soak in the hot tub. How does that sound?"

Maynard didn't try to hide the desire in his eyes, and neither did Jenna.

"Sounds like a slice of heaven in the middle of hell," Jenna said. "Absolutely perfect." She took his arm in hers and dragged him toward the door.

"Bye, Wile-E," Jenna said. "Call us if you need us."

EPILOGUE

TOP SECRET MEMORANDUM

TO: Queen Antares, Captain Aleksander Kharritov

FROM: Yuan Tee Mining Industries, Corporate HQ, President Gary Jackson

REF: Ross 128b Mining Colony Emergency Extraction

DATE: July 28, 2177

Primary Objective: Retrieve cargo from planet surface.

Cargo Designation: Alien ship of unknown origin.

Metal: Unknown composition.

Potential Value: Astronomical

Secondary Objective: Extract any Surviving Colonists

Special Orders: All colonists are expendable, if necessary, to achieve Primary Objective.

To Be Continued …

ABOUT THE AUTHOR

Mike was a cop for almost 12 years, but the last 13 years he's been teaching Military, Law Enforcement and Bodyguards high speed, tactical and off-road driving as well as hand to hand Combatives. He enjoys martial arts and has been a practitioner since 1989 of various styles. Filipino blade arts are his current favorite. Since he was a teenager he's loved reading, writing, and watching movies, particularly in the horror and sci-fi genre. He's also been a prolific reader of theology and studied quite extensively for a layman. He has a beautiful wife who is very supportive and a son and daughter who are both graduated. His babies now are a German Shepherd named Ziva, a Daddy's girl who loves to play... even when he's writing, and a Border Collie mix named Joey "The Bandit" who will steal anything and everything he can, even the toys right out of Ziva's mouth. Mike is a lover of music, as well, and it is an integral part of his writing ritual.

Mike writes an eclectic mix of horror stories. He explores dark supernatural entities, cosmic terrors, and natural monstrosities. However, the wicked deeds the human heart can conceive and inflict on others as well as our capacity to act against such things pervades much of his work. According to Chris Hall, at DLS Reviews, Mike is "a master of utterly uncompromising hardboiled revenge-thrillers." He has a way of provoking a significant response from his readers – whether shock, terror, dread, an uneasy sense of empathy, Heebie Jeebie crawlies or surprise at unexpected twists. Mike will *make* you feel while you read his words. As one reviewer said, when you read a Mike Duke book you don't just read about an experience, you *have* an experience.

Mike's novels LOW and Where the Gods Sleep as well as his Ashley's Tale Trilogy (Ashley's Tale, Making Jake and The Initiation) are published by Stitched Smile Publications. Mike's novellas Hate Inexorable, CRAWL, Warm Dark Places Are Best, The Yuletide Butcher, and Fear the Gods are self-published. He currently has short stories published in over ten different anthologies with more to come. In addition to these published works, he provides short stories, flash fiction, poetry and flash-non-fiction on his Patreon page for fans who can't get enough of what the Duke of Horror is serving up.

Links:

AMAZON AUTHOR PAGE

PATREON PAGE

Made in the USA
Middletown, DE
13 December 2024

66882950R00086